MW00719810

The Flowers of Reminiscence

Ronnie Ray Jenkins

The Larry Czerwonka Company
Hawaii

This is a work of fiction. Names, characters, businesses, places, events and incidents are either the products of the author's imagination or used in a fictitious manner. Any resemblance to actual persons, living or dead, or actual events is purely coincidental

Copyright © 2012 Ronnie Ray Jenkins

All rights reserved.

ISBN: 0615611907
ISBN-13: 978-0615611907

DEDICATION

For my sister, Vivian,
Our Sunday phone calls meant a great deal to me, and I remember
with great fondness reading to you from this book each week. Sadly,
we never reached the end. Know now you are at peace, and that your
memory will live on.

CONTENTS

CONTENTS

ACKNOWLEDGMENTS

There are those that believe in succeeding, and know how to do it. One person stands out, Larry Czerwonka, owner of The Larry Czerwonka Company in Hawaii. He followed my writing for more than six years without wavering. He made this happen, and I thank you for that, Larry. This is just the beginning.

Loren Lilly, thanks for your helpful insight, and making me see past the words.

My wife and kids for hanging in there to see this happen, and for teaching an impatient man, patience.

Finally, for all the Nellie Blue Bells out there, I will always remember your existence.

THE COVER ART

A pact was made more than twenty-six years ago between two college friends. We'd not forget each other's dreams and goals. I would like to thank David Olk of Mount Vernon, Ohio for his drawing that became the cover of this book. His folk art lives on, and he can be contacted on Facebook @ David Olk Originals www.facebook.com/pages/David-Olk-Originals/304653872930052

ONE
SOWING THE SEEDS

Nellie Blue Bell toiled once more to reminisce on this chilly night, which found her once again, sitting in a chair made familiar to her aged body by the passing of time. It seemed to her that her old brain was a ball of bread dough requiring kneading to attempt to recollect or draw out memories hidden deep within the recesses. The months passed slowly in those long hours of thought. Still, she found herself no closer to an answer. She questioned why it had happened to her, but refused to indulge in self-pity tonight.

She thought, and revisited, how the handyman back at her home in West Virginia tacked down that annoying piece of carpet covering the treads of the worn stairs. Frowning in thought, the lines on her face grew deep. She nearly always used the rail leading upstairs as an added precaution. The well-traveled steps creaked the years with her footsteps; so many times in fact she wore a path in the old carpet.

Sure, there were the odd few times she stumbled. But she would catch herself, and pause on the staircase to allow her panicked heart to return to normal. Old people did that, but what puzzled her most was recollecting a hand on her back, a sharp blow. She shook her head as if she would jar loose a thought and return back to that particular day in West Virginia. Aged minds can play tricks. Still, with each night of thought, she felt sure she had not stumbled or tripped. Who would have done this to her and, more importantly, why would they? To make matters worse, nobody around here seemed to listen to her. She was alone in this god-forsaken place, and forced by circumstance to call Beacon Manor, home..

The howling wind rattled the windows of the nursing home, drawing her attention outside. Tree branches cast swaying shadows against the manicured lawn and nearly empty parking lot. The light from the tall poles surrounding the lot bathed the few, parked cars in a marmalade glow. Even the fragile limbs of the crape myrtles seemed to be painted with thick orange Jell-O.

Crossed branches, scratching in the wind, clawed upward for non-existent sunlight. Like those very trees, Nellie always reached skyward fighting for the better things in life. Instead, they had put her out to pasture at Beacon Manor, a nursing home tucked away in some Texas town, far away from her beloved West Virginia.

Gazing around the room from her seat, she inventoried her meager belongings. A few pictures, some jewelry, and her book of pressed flowers were all the mementos thrown into a cardboard box, as if they were going to be set on the curb for recycling.

Her West Virginia home for sixty years was gone now, its contents long emptied and sold by two "jackals", as Nellie often called them. Still, she was grateful, she thought: At least being here saved her from having to watch the garage sale vultures make their final swoop to pick clean the few remaining scraps of her life.

Her thin fingers stroked the worn fabric covering the chair's arm as raindrops hit the window's glass with whispered taps. Rubber wheels, squeaking in the hallway, drew near to her room. A gruff voice mercifully interrupted the thoughts of her lost home.

"It's time for your medicine, Nellie."

A stainless steel cart rattled through the doorway, followed by a tired tall woman who clasped the handle like a shopping cart. Snatching the pen tucked behind her ear, she scratched something on a chart.

"This will help you sleep."

Every night they came with the pills: Tonight was no exception. Nellie looked at the cup, and her sour expression deepened the wrinkles on her thin drawn face.

"I really don't care for any tonight."

She shifted on the cushion, searching for the familiar indentation that provided some comfort for her aching bones.

"It's doctor's orders, Sweetie," the nurse said, patting her on the shoulder. Nellie grimaced: They always touched, prodded, and probed, and there was no getting used to it.

She bent forward obediently as if taking communion. Her shaking hand weakly clamped the cup as pills rattled the clear plastic bottom of it. The pills slid onto her dry tongue, and she winced at the bitterness of the powder that was dusted on the capsules. The routine did not require eye contact when she exchanged the empty for another. Luke warm water splashed her tongue, loosening the sticky gelatin capsules, and she swallowed easily. It was all habit now, and she knew the drill.

"Would you like some help into bed?" asked the nurse.

"No, thank you. I am going to stay up until midnight. I want to usher in spring," Nellie sunk defeated back into the chair with a sorrowful sigh.

"It might be my last you know."

"Now stop that nonsense," the nurse said, bending over the cart to replace a brown plastic pitcher among the cups of pills, bandages, and syringes.

Nellie knew the pills worked fast, and already the nurse's uniform seemed to shimmer with radiant heat waves. She hoped she could fight the effects until after midnight. The nurse jotted something on the chart and disappeared to continue her rounds. Her gruff voice drifted up the hall, warning the next patient she was on her way.

Fighting heavy eyelids with combative blinks, Nellie looked around the room. This was the place she had called home for the last eighteen months. She thought of it as her square box, and considered it only slightly better than a jail cell.

There were those four walls painted a dull green, with chips of random peeling paint. The tiled ceiling was yellowed, and several tiles hung loose, warped and water stained. A single door led to the hallway and, just to the right of that entrance, the door to her bathroom. A chest of drawers by her bed, and a nightstand all in matching pressed fiberboard, did little to heighten the ambiance of her surroundings. A comforter of pink and blue flowers covered her single bed. Burnt orange curtains, covering the two squared windows beside her chair, sarcastically complemented the entire décor.

From her chair, Nellie could look out into the hallway, and view the nurses and aides performing their duties. The thin walls did little to muffle the sounds at night. Her room, sandwiched between the noisiest of the patients, was just another unlucky draw according to her.

Out her door and to the right was Mr. Banks' room, a veteran of the Great War. Some nights he ventured back to France and, when he did, all hell followed. His window shaking screams of Krauts advancing on their position usually woke her with a start. Three days after she arrived, he stuck his head in her door and ordered her to put on her gas mask. The Krauts were gassing them again. In his more coherent times, he told her, his greatest regret was never meeting General Pershing.

To the left of Nellie's room, Gertie Martz served up heaping plates of a different audible torture. She retired after nearly fifty years of teaching. Now she held classes when the mood struck her. Her voice filled the halls as she lectured invisible students with state capitals, times tables, and geography lessons. Geography lessons ultimately resulted in the mention of France, providing the cue for ex-private Gordon Banks to swing into action. Soon, he would yell from his room, and sometimes from his bed, "Viva La France!"

Nellie glanced at the watch on her slim wrist, dappled with age spots. Midnight neared and spring would arrive in a few minutes. Spring reminded her again of home and how much she loved that time of year back there. She looked out at the spattering drops slapping the pavement of the black parking lot. The concentric rings, forming in the growing puddles, moved outward with each new raindrop. At least the rain is good for the flowers, she thought.

Midnight passed with the same tranquilized slowness that numbingly had her rising from the chair. Her walker was within reach, so she steadied herself and, with her right hand, grasped it and slid it toward her. The rubber tips scraped the floor with mouse-like squeaks. She held on for a moment, and then shuffled across the room to her bed. The night aide would close her door. She was just too tired from the pills to bother.

She peeled the comforter down, and pulled herself up on the small bed. A glass of water sat on the nightstand. The pills left her mouth as dry as wadded cotton, and she picked up the glass, drinking until the water dripped down her chin and on to the front of her blue, cotton housecoat.

She set the cup back on her nightstand, shut off the table lamp, and rolled over on her back. The light from the hallway entered the room and bathed her wrinkled face in yellow. She grew tired and lulled to the precipice of sleep with a rhythmic, "three plus three is nine, three plus four is twelve, three plus five is..." Mrs. Martz was teaching again, confusing addition with multiplication.

With the exception of the multiplication lesson in Mrs. Martz's room, it was an unusually quiet night. A rerun of the Dick Van Dyke show played on the floor model television in the lounge area. Nellie heard the gruff-voiced nurse laughing and then remembered the old show: Rob probably tripped over the ottoman, she thought. She also thought that if she could remember the show and Rob, then maybe, just maybe, she could somehow pull the lost memories from her tired old mind. She just might solve this mystery of how she ended up here.

* * *

Nellie woke early. The sounds of the cooks preparing breakfast, once again, disturbed her sleep. For the last eighteen months, the banging and clanging of the stainless steel pots and pans, the rattling of silverware, and the clinking of dishes, were her wake up call.

She looked at the cheap, white, plastic clock on her nightstand and wondered why she bothered setting the thing, as she fumbled to find the button. Not once since her arrival did she give it a chance to do the duty of waking her at 6:00. She pushed the comforter off, dangling her bony white legs over the edge of the bed with her feet poised over a pair of slippers. After two attempts, she managed to get her feet into the fleece-lined footwear, given to her as a gift from her only daughter. That was the last time she had seen her.

Squinting, she reached for the aluminum walker. She swiped and swatted at it twice before finally connecting. She hated being old, and she still had not adjusted to the hip replacement. Standing for a moment, she let her stiff body adapt.

She shuffled to the door leading to the hallway and opened it. Mrs. Martz's snores ripped through the halls like an idling chainsaw. Nellie imagined her jowls flapping with each breath as she let the door close again. She flipped on the overhead light and slowly made it to the closet, opened it, and chose a pink flowered housedress from her sparse collection. Perfect for the first day of spring, she thought.

Opening the bathroom door, she worked her way inside, leaving her walker near the door. Handicapped bars jutted out from the wall behind the toilet: Reminders, she thought, of her limitations. Moving to the tub, she filled it, checking the water temperature with her hand. She was grateful she could bathe herself. The woman in Room 9 screamed each time they bathed her.

While the tub filled, Nellie made her way back into the room without the aid of her walker. She only used it when her old body played insubordination with her mind. Sometimes the weather would wreak havoc with her arthritis and hip, but most times, she tried her best not to use the thing.

Returning to the bathroom with a towel and washcloth, she undressed and grasped the safety bars. She lowered herself into the water, and for a few minutes, rested, allowing the warm water to soak into her tired old muscles. Leaning her head back, she closed her eyes and remembered her bathroom in the house back home. She wished for its warm coziness with the knickknacks and magazine rack made by her grandfather. The floor length mirror trimmed in brass, the one from the magazine that she scrimped and saved to buy, came to mind. She wondered who had it now. She especially liked the wooden sink with the brass faucet and the marble water basin. She missed it all.

She was in love with that old place and it nearly killed her when her daughter sold it, promising that the proceeds would go for her care. Barbara, her own flesh and blood, had the nerve to marry the lawyer who handled the paperwork putting her here. She clenched the washcloth tight in her hand. Was he the third, or the fourth husband? She could not remember. There had been so many men in the girl's life.

"Miss Nellie, it's time for breakfast. Are you okay?," asked her favorite aide, Elaina. Nellie felt she was the only person who seemed to give a "fiddler's damn" about her. She was the first aide Nellie met when they wheeled her in this place. In eighteen months, they grew close, and Elaina was now more of a daughter to her than Barbara.

"I'll be down in twenty minutes, Elaina," Nellie said loudly. She slowly hoisted herself up and stepped like a careful flamingo from the tub. Standing in front of the mirror, she dried herself off.

She brushed her short white hair and gazed at her reflection. Over seventy years of aging and her blue eyes had not lost their depth. With just the right light, tiny specks of silver reflected and danced playfully inside her irises. She tilted her head left and right and tried to see if they would do it. For a moment, she swore they danced with the life of a young girl again. She dressed for breakfast, and walked to the dining room. Her shoulders drooped as she entered and noticed the only open seat available.

"You look real pretty today, Mademoiselle," Mr. Banks said. He winked as he slid the chair out for her. Standing at parade rest, he waited until she sat down. She ignored his compliment and took a drink of the weak coffee in front of her. It is not that she did not like Mr. Banks, but he did have a reputation for being a little too "touchy-feely" as she put it. She inched her chair a comfortable distance from him.

Fingering her napkin nervously, she watched as the aides went from table to table and placed plates of food in front of each resident according to their diet. A woman with gray hair, missing in fistful size spots, screamed that she could not eat cold cereal; it would give her a heart attack. She had said that, religiously, every morning for the past eighteen months.

"Pipe down," commanded Mr. Banks, "You'll give away our position."

The woman stopped yelling, as she did every morning upon receiving Banks' command.

Nellie concentrated on the tasteless, rubbery, scrambled eggs. The bacon was overdone and the toast was cold. She wished she were back in her own kitchen. She remembered how she baked and cooked in it. That smell of home-baked bread would fill the house. Oh, how she missed that. She slid the plate back and swallowed the last of her coffee. As she got up to leave, a hand patted her backside. Banks smiled at her, adding a crisp salute. Disgusted, she wrinkled her nose at him and went back to her room.

Once inside, she spotted the cardboard box in the corner. She rummaged through it and smiled when, at the bottom, she found it. How could she have missed finding it after all these months? She wrote it off as boredom turning into a more thorough search. Making her way across the room, she sat down.

She leaned toward the window and pulled open the curtains. Sunshine streamed into the dull room. Out across the lot, jonquils flowered at the base of the crape myrtles and their cream colored petals bowed slightly. A breeze combed through the grass like invisible fingers, parting the blades.

She turned, directing her gaze to the book resting on her lap and ran her fingers across the ivory cloth covering. A lacy half-inch border surrounded the book's cover. She caressed the lace and silently read the needlepoint words on the front: To Nellie, from Mother and Father, April 10, 1901.

Her mother, pregnant with Nellie, had sewn the cover and, after her birth, needle pointed the date. Through the years, Nellie had added flowers, carefully pressing them between the pages. Events worthy to be included were inscribed underneath each flower. The four-inch thick book held no less than seventy-four years of memories.

Gently pinching the upper corner, she folded the cover over to the first page and gingerly brushed the dried bluebell with her fingertip. The petals were crisp and dry, and the blue color had faded. Her mother had written in flowing letters at the bottom of the page, "Your first flower. Daddy picked it at the springhouse and gave you the middle name of Blue."

Nellie gazed upon the words, the ink still black and contrasting to the yellowed and brittle page. She thought of the woman whose fingers had held the pen, and imagined her dipping the nib in the inkwell. How careful she must have been not to drip any of the ink onto the pages. She touched the flower again, and closed her eyes. She could see him in her mind picking the flower at the bubbling spring, and remembered her father.

TWO
BLUE BELLS AND BIRTH

The gunshots echoed across the mountains, bouncing from hill to hill, and down through the town. It was New Years Eve 1901 in Appalachian country, with hard-working men, drunk on flaming hot moonshine, homemade beer, and wine, celebrating noisily. There would be no labor tomorrow in the mines; only the work of nursing a good old, well earned, New Years Day hangover.

Harmon Bell stood out on his back porch and placed the twelve-gauge shotgun's stock tight against his muscular shoulder. He aimed high in the direction of a constellation, its name unknown to him. With a steady squeeze, the shotgun exploded, throwing flame and orange sparks two feet out from the barrels. It kicked his shoulder like one of his mules and left him stumbling back, followed by a white cloud of acrid smoke.

"Happy New Year!" he yelled drunkenly, his deep voice directed to the star dotted sky.

Harmon celebrated, along with most of the town, from his house perched high on the side of the mountain. He preferred distance. The gunshots grew silent, replaced with happy fiddle music drifting up from below.

"Harmon?" He ignored the soft voice musically drifting out to him from inside the house.

He had been married for a year now, had a pregnant wife who was due in about four months, and took care of the mules for seven local mines. To him, life could not be any better.

"Harmon. It's nearly one o'clock. Get in here."

"Coming," he said disappointedly.

He grabbed his half-empty bottle of homebrew off the rough railing and went inside. She was sitting in a wooden rocking chair by the coal stove with a worn wool blanket draped across her lap. The coal oil lamps flickered in the room and the wood-stove added a warm coziness to the place. He grinned at her sheepishly. Not many women told Harmon Bell what to do, but she was the exception.

"Happy New Year," he said, leaning over her and stroking her swollen belly. She looked up, placing the palm of her hand flat on the side of his face, gently stroking his thick beard. Anna Bell was nineteen years old and proud to be his wife. He was a hard worker and a good provider. Underneath that devil-may-care attitude that he portrayed, she knew he was a kind, loving, and compassionate man.

"I picked out a name," she whispered. He moved to sit down in a dark cloth chair that was plump with horsehair, bits of it sticking out through a tear in the arm. Leaning toward her, he took a long pull off the bottle.

"Ya don't know if it's gonna be a girl or a boy," his soft, deep voice seemed to help warm the room.

"I know that dummy," she said, her voice ringing soft with a hint of a Southern twang.

"Nellie, if it's a girl, and Harmon, if it's a boy," she said.

The thought of a boy made him happy, but he hid his excitement behind the upturned bottle. His dark eyes peered from behind it.

Her blonde hair was long and draped down the front of her chest. She had blue eyes and light skin, features inherited from her Swedish mother's side of the family.

Harmon pushed up from the chair and, with weaving steps, walked to the coal stove. While he noisily tended the fire, her eyes followed his every move. She always considered him ruggedly handsome, with his mop of black hair and his beard as black as the coal he shoveled into the firebox. He had those dark eyes, mysterious and piercing, or soulful and compassionate, depending on the mood.

He closed the stove's door and a small cloud of black smoke rolled up the lip of the door toward the ceiling, coating the sparse furniture with soot. Her constant dusting just pushed it around to land on something else. Sauntering back to the chair, he finished the bottle of home brew. He turned the big bottle over in his hands, looking remorseful.

"It's late," she said. The fiddle music down below died at the same time his bottle did, and he agreed with her.

A short time later in the big bed, the combination of her closeness, the heavy quilts, and the homebrew warmed him more than he liked. He tossed about, finally rolling to face her.

"I get to pick the middle name, right?" he said.

"Yeah, I promised you when we first found out."

"Well, I have one. I don't know if you'll like it though," Harmon said.

"Just tell me," she pleaded. "I'm tired and I won't laugh too much if it's really dumb." Her soft giggle teased him into replying.

"Blue."

"The color?" She questioned him in the dimness.

"Naw, it has to do with the flowers and our last name," he said.

Anna propped her head up on her hand and looked into his eyes. She bit her bottom lip trying hard not to laugh.

"Well, I'm waiting…….."

"You know the blue bells that come up every April down by the springhouse?"

She concentrated on his serious face. She would not laugh at his choice of names, no matter how bad she wanted to, or how bad her bottom lip was hurting from stifling her giggles.

"I like it," she said, "now kiss me, and go to sleep."

Harmon kissed her and rolled to face the nightstand. He lowered the wick on the lamp, drawing a curtain of black over the room. His elbow gently nudged her when she laughed in the dark.

* * *

April brought rain and the heavy winter snows melted. Harmon stood on the front porch looking down from his mountaintop. The church, the feed mill, and twenty or so company houses made up the town. The coal companies owned them and rented the small wooden houses to the miners. They stood side by side with barely enough room for a small garden, he thought. Harmon appreciated that he did not have to pay the six dollars a month rent to live in one of the company houses, and vowed he never would.

The biggest building was the company store, whitewashed like all the houses, but with "Belton Mines Company Store" in bold black letters emblazoned across the front. The newly opened bank was the only brick building in the town and he watched the workman as they cleaned up the last few bricks left from their work.

Harmon's view seemed to stretch for miles. The mountains on the other side of the town rose up and gray clouds drifted slowly across their tree-covered faces. His seclusion was preferred and allowed him the opportunity to take game from his front porch, if he chose.

He watched two wagons pulled by a team of horses move onto the lot of the feed mill, and several men loaded them with plump, burlap sacks of feed. The distance afforded faint sounds of the thumping sacks on hollow wood, and the voices of the men. The only clear sound from below was the church bell ringing. It rang every Sunday morning at nine. Harmon took out his pocket watch and adjusted the time. He did it every Sunday.

"Harmon," Anna called with urgency from inside the house.

He quickly walked inside and straight to the bedroom, finding Anna propped up on the bed. Plumped feather pillows stuffed between the headboard and her back helped her sit. Droplets of beaded sweat on her forehead glistened on her smooth skin.

"It's time," she said, "You better get Doc Owens up here." Her voice trembled and he noticed she was clutching her stomach with both hands.

He regretted not bringing the midwife up here a week ago, but Anna did not want that. She thought she had at least until the end of the month. Her moans sent him scrambling out of the bedroom.

"I'm leaving right now," he yelled over his shoulder. His heart pounded as he dashed to the door, flinging it open. He ignored the porch steps and leaped well out into the wet yard.

Running to the pole barn in the back, he slipped, falling in the mud. Jumping to his feet, he slid toward the big doors of the barn. Grasping his fastest horse by the bridle, he quickly hitched it to the wagon backed inside the barn.

Grabbing the reins one handed, he cracked the whip with his right hand across the horse's flanks. The horse lunged through the doorway slipping in the foot deep mud. The wagon creaked and rocked, fighting to pull free from the sucking grip. The whip cut the air, and the horse's footing held. Harmon urged the horse on with the biting whip. Its trot changed to an outstretched gallop that flung chunks of black mud from its hooves.

Doc Owens was at the church and, after getting his bag at his office, they reached the house with only minutes to spare. It was then that Nellie Blue Bell, gasped, wailed, and took her first breath of West Virginia air. Harmon Bell always said that when she was born the rain stopped, and it had. The sun actually appeared for a few minutes, long enough for him to walk down to the springhouse and pick a bouquet of the blue bells without getting drenched.

Nearly five weeks after her birth, his excitement had never waned. "Leave her sleep," Anna said softly from her chair by the stove. "I swear you're always fooling with her."

She looked up from her stitching of the date on the book. "There, all finished," she said, holding the book up for him and showing off her handiwork. Harmon nodded his approval, returning his gaze to the cradle where Nellie slept.

"She looks just like you," he said.

"Come here," she patted the cushion next to her on the new couch he bought last week. He sat near her and she took his hands in hers, rubbing the rough skin, and moving her hand up the muscles of his strong forearms.

"We haven't had much time alone. Have we?"

"Not really, but you know I have to get the addition finished on the barn and all. That new mining company is coming in July and my guess is they will need at least twenty mules, maybe more, for hauling. I gotta make room for them."

"I just wish you would slow down some. Maybe just a little bit." Her pleading blue eyes flickered.

"When the barn is finished, I'm gonna hire me a couple of hands and they can do the feeding and cleaning, that way all I'll have to do is count the money." His thick black eyebrows rose slightly with his laugh.

"Promise?" She asked.

"Promise."

* * *

By July, with the expansion of the barn complete and the Bell's two hired hands looking after the mules, Harmon concentrated on other business. He bought twenty more acres of land on the other side of the spring and, now, between him and the bank, owned two hundred and two acres.

He cleared timber and planted buckwheat and alfalfa. The mules had plenty of room to graze. McCoy Brothers Mining Company opened up two new mines and Harmon landed the contract. He borrowed from the bank and bought twenty-seven more mules.

* * *

By the beginning of September, Harmon was able to spend the time he had promised with Anna and Nellie. One Saturday they took the buggy over to Charleston and spent the night in a hotel. For the first time, they experienced hot and cold running water and an inside toilet that did not have to be emptied down the hole of the outhouse.

September passed, leaving nights that brought the chilled mountain air swooping to the front door of the Bell's house. Harmon finished shoveling the last of the coal in the cellar. He wanted to be ready for the winter that would be upon them quicker than desired. He recalled watching a wooly worm caterpillar, crawling up the barn door two weeks ago, and it had been almost completely black. Everyone in these hills knew that the blacker they were, the rougher the winter was going to be.

Anna appeared from around the side of the house with Nellie wrapped in a blanket. Harmon stood leaning on the shovel, sweat dripping off his face and smudges of coal dust on his forehead left from wiping his face with his sleeve.

"Here," she said, holding out a glass of lemonade. He drank it fast, wincing with the headache caused by the cold drink.

"Don't drink it so fast and that won't happen," she said.

He ignored her remark, instead answering, "Well, for once I feel like I'm ahead of the game." He reached out to lift the blanket from Nellie's face.

"Just look at those hands," Anna said. She directed a playful slap to his outstretched hand, and twisted the squirming bundle away from him. "I just bathed her and I don't want her covered with coal dust like her Daddy."

"Coal is all in baby girl," he said, directing his soft tone to the bundle. "We'll be nice and warm this winter."

"By the way, I have your bath water ready too, Mister."

"I surely could use one."

He wiped his hands down the front of his coal-dusted denim overalls.

"Well, let's go in, it's a little too chilly out here for her anyway," she said.

The three of them walked around the house and went inside. Anna put Nellie in her cradle and picked up the clothes that Harmon left lay in a heap by the galvanized steel washtub in the kitchen. She handed him a bar of lye soap with one hand and threw the dirty clothes on top of the ones already piled in the corner of the kitchen. She shook her head at the mountain of laundry and wished she had a crank washer. The way things were going for them it wouldn't be long, she thought, as she ducked underneath the rope that stretched from one end of the kitchen to the other and hung heavy with drying cloth diapers and dungarees. The cool weather took days for them to dry outside.

Harmon leaned back in the tub. The warmth soaked into his aching muscles. Today, he shoveled in eight more tons of coal on top of the seven from yesterday. It was beginning to get dark and Anna walked through the house lighting the coal oil lamps while he bathed.

In the kitchen, she lit the lamp on top of the dark oak icebox. She took a package of venison wrapped in white butcher's paper from inside the icebox and plopped it into a pan on the big, black, wood-burning cook stove. Lifting the heavy round cast iron lid off the top with the lifter, she balanced it with one hand while she picked up a stick of wood stacked nearby. A shower of orange sparks spewed upward as the stick of wood landed heavily in the bottom of the stove.

"Supper will be ready in about an hour," she said over the noisy rattle of the metallic grating as the griddle stubbornly slid onto the lip of the hole.

"Good, I'm starved," he yelled above the splashing as he ran his hands through the water, attempting to create suds. Harmon scrubbed his body with the heavy, wooden handled brush, the bristles making his skin tingle and leaving red streaks. He quickly dipped his head between his legs into the soapy water, wetting his hair and whipping his black mane backwards. Droplets of water sprayed leaving a speckled wet trail from the ceiling, and down the side of the wall. Blindly he ran his hands through the water, searching for the sunken bar of soap.

"Anna," he yelled. His eyelids squeezed tightly shut and water dripping down his broad back. He called her again.

"Yes, Harmon?"

"Could you find the soap for me? I have water in my eyes, and I'll be damned if I can find it." Water dripped off his black hair and beard, trickling back into the tub from the tip of his beard.

She leaned over the tub and ran her hand back and forth searching all the way to the bottom. He watched her with one squinting eye. Suddenly, he grabbed her wrists with his strong hands and pulled her into the tub. She landed gasping and screaming between his legs with her back against his chest.

"Harmon Blandon Bell!" she said, "I can't believe you." The bar of soap slid from his fingers and plopped into the water, for he had been holding it the entire time.

He pulled her back toward him, lifting her long blonde tresses flowing down the back of her wet dress and floating where they met the water. Gently, he gathered her hair up with both hands and raised it off her back allowing it to drape over her right shoulder. He kissed the back of her thin neck, softly brushing his beard back and forth against her skin.

She slid back, pressing her shoulders against his heaving chest. She felt his hands moving under the water pulling the cloth up and over her hips, her back, and shoulders. Her dress landed on the floor with a wet smack.

His arms wrapped around her thin waist and she felt his tickling fingers just above the band of her bloomers. He hooked his thumbs between her skin and the wet cotton. The bloomers slipped over her hips toward her ankles, and wound up dangling off the toes of her right foot. She bent her ankle downward and the bloomers slid to the floor.

She felt his rough hands on the backs of her legs, slowly lifting her up, and pulling her back toward him. With her legs bent and her feet on either side of the metal tub, he gently lowered her on to him. The water sloshed over the tub as he held her waist and lifted her up and down. He pushed upward to meet her each time, nearly lifting her naked body completely out of the water.

His hands moved to her firm, white breasts, cupping one in each hand. She bucked wildly, and twisted her head to meet his lips. Grabbing her chin with his right hand, he helped her to reach his waiting mouth. Her soft moaning increased as she shuddered

16

violently and collapsed with her head pressed against his chest. She snuggled closer, listening as the soft lapping water kept time with the beating of his heart.

It was nearly nine o'clock when they went to bed. The thunder woke Harmon sometime around midnight. Brilliant flashes of lightning lit the room. Anna slept undisturbed by the racket. It amazed him how she had ever heard Nellie all those nights.

The storm blew across the top of the mountain. Wind whistled through the trees, shaking the house. He cocked his ear toward the window and listened as the rain began to pelt the tarred roof. A blinding flash, a second or two, then the deafening boom of the thunder pounded hollow through the room. He listened for Nellie. She slept as sound as her mother did, he thought.

All around, bolts of lightning wickedly stabbed at the earth, one of them striking the weather vane on the new addition of the pole barn. The white heat seared a dry wooden board along the copper pole attached to the side of the barn. The sweet fragrance of wood smoke filled the air. The copper pole, meant to carry the electrical devil to the bowels of the earth, now heated the side of the barn to its kindling temperature. Bits of hay and straw, sticking through the cracks and touching the pole, glowed red-orange.

Inside the barn, the nervous animals snorted. They crowded each other, huddling for a moment, and then pushed off in confusion. They lifted their soft muzzles in the air with expanding nostrils, testing for smoke. Their strong flanks twitched as they do when the horseflies come in season. A few of the larger animals stomped their hooves on the dirt floor, creating dull thuds that vibrated the packed soil, warning the others.

The wind came again, this time igniting the straw and hay. Dry grain dust circulating on the top floor of the barn exploded. Glowing red-hot embers, as big as walnuts, fell through the wide cracks of the upper floor, branding the backs of the mules and horses below. The animals tossed their heads frantically. Fearful eyes rolled back to the whites as they realized there was no escape.

Harmon, close to sleep earlier, was now jarred wide-awake. He spied an orange reflection on the window's glass. His forehead wrinkled at the puzzling sight, and then it dawned on him it was coming from the barn. He threw off the quilts and shook Anna awake.

"What....what is it?" she asked.

"I think the barn--the barn is on fire," he said anxiously, while frantically pulling on his boots. He tore through the dark house, blindly crashing into furniture. Nellie's cry followed when his searching hands smashed an oil lamp. He flung the door open and ran across the back yard. Desperate whinnies and braying filled the night.

Flames and sparks shot upward from a hole burned in the barn's roof. The wind carried embers toward the tarred roof of the house. Harmon turned to it, but the screeching of the second floor beams found him pulling on the double doors of the barn. The outer walls of the barn shook with the thundering kicks of the mules. A crossbeam fell and the second floor collapsed dumping a year's supply of straw and grain, feeding the hungry fire. The wooden doors bulged outward with the pressure of the weight from inside. The metal bar on the outside door twisted in the hasp with such force that it bent out, locking everything inside the barn. Harmon felt helpless and turned his attention to the house.

Anna stood frozen on the porch, silhouetted against the wall by the red glow and flashes of lightning. His eyes opened wide when he looked above her and saw a circle of flame near the chimney licking away at the tarred roof.

His legs were rubber as he ran toward her. Struggling to breathe, the pain never registered from the burns on his hands, face, and back. Debris was falling from the barn's roof as he turned to head for the house.

"Get the baby!" he screamed at her. She stood wide-eyed and in shock.

He rushed past her, hitting the front door with great force, tearing the door from the hinges, leaving it cockeyed against the living room wall. Dashing to the cradle, he scooped it and the baby up in his arms. He never felt the cooked skin rip off the palms of his hands and dangle limply off the rockers of the cradle.

He ran outside across the yard and, when he thought he was a safe distance away, gently lowered the cradle to the ground. He ran back toward the house and looked up onto the roof. It was an inferno. Anna stared straight ahead, mesmerized. He grabbed her roughly by the shoulders and shook her violently.

"Anna, Anna!" he screamed, just inches from her face. She continued to stare past him, through him. He pulled his hand back and swung it through the air. It cracked on her cheek like a pistol shot. She blubbered, like someone drowning.

"We need to save some things. We don't have much time for God's sake."

He pulled her by the hand and they went inside, grabbing blankets, and throwing their prized possessions in a few wooden empty dynamite boxes. Quickly he scanned the room. By the coal stove, he picked up the flower book and threw it into the box. Next, he picked up the clock and a few figurines they brought from their trip to Charleston. The creaking from upstairs warned him to move faster.

Anna picked up one of the boxes and ran outside with it. Seeing the cradle, she ran to it, falling on the wet ground beside it. She put her hands over her ears to drown out the bellowing cries of the animals. The sickening odor of burning hair and flesh, carried on the wind, drifted past her nose.

"HARMON!," she screamed.

He stumbled to the doorway, and staggered through the yard to collapse on the ground beside her. She rolled over and fell onto his chest sobbing. The coal lamps exploded with loud pops. They watched as the roof caved in. The pelting rain cooled his burned face as he lay on his back, his outstretched arms as if being prepared for crucifixion. In a sense, he may as well been sentenced to it.

As the sun rose, he walked around the foundation and stared at the coal, still smoldering red and smelling of sulphur. Everything was gone. Through the backyard, he stopped at the charred remains of the barn. The carcasses of the animals littered the ground. Some were obscenely bloated with burned legs pointing upwards toward the sky. He stared at his horse that lay sprawled on its swollen belly, its legs splayed out from under it and its mouth wide open. It lay close to the charred water trough. Two empty sockets stared back at him.

Folks below had spotted the flames last night and had finally reached the house. By that time, all that remained was the foundation. In Harmon's quest for solitude, he had neglected to realize that the town bucket brigade would never make it in time.

Now, with Anna and Nellie safely housed in the church, he walked up the muddy road to survey the damage at the house.

The coal stove and cook stove had both ended up in heap of metal rubble in what used to be the cellar. The intense heat had fused together anything glass into one misshapen marble.

The large beams still crackled and smoldered. The smell of the burned animals made his stomach churn when a brief gust of wind sent a reminder his way. Like a beaten prizefighter, with his hands wrapped in white bandages the size of boxing gloves, he turned, leaving behind his dream.

THREE
CARNATIONS AND COAL

Time passed, and five-year old Nellie waited by the door, peering out through the screen into the street. He was almost to the house. She heard him whistling before she saw him, and in just a moment she would hear the familiar sound of his work boots thumping on the wooden porch. She moved from the screen door to hide behind the white, solid wood door that swung inward.

The silvery round metal lunch box clanged as he set it down on the porch. She cocked her ear, peering with one big blue eye through the crack of the doorframe. Taking a deep breath, she waited for the familiar screeching noise of the spring pulling the screen door shut.

She watched him trying to hide his smile, acting as if he didn't expect her to jump from behind the door as soon as he stepped inside. She did this every time he worked day shift. He played along and she thought that it surprised him each time. It was their game. The door swung open and she jumped out with a loud, "Boo!" He grabbed his chest and took a step backward as she laughed loud, revealing her straight white teeth.

Jumping and dancing around his legs, she told him about the puppy the neighbors found earlier down by the creek. She followed at his heels as he walked to the kitchen table and slumped into a chair. She crawled up into his lap and began stroking his cheek.

His face felt rough on her fingertips and she traced the scars on his right cheek and chin, touching the permanent reminders of the fire. He would never be able to grow a full beard again. He tried once, but it was bare in the spots where the heat destroyed the follicles. She didn't care: It was her Daddy and she thought he was the most handsome man in the world.

The screen door opened and Harmon turned to see Anna crossing the living room with an armful of clothes. She tossed them on the couch.

"All done," she said, walking over and placing a kiss on Harmon's cheek.

"I had to pick up a new clothesline down at Belton's today. The old one was broken in so many places I couldn't tie it up anymore." She had her long hair pinned up on her head and the back of her neck was pink with sunburn. Her long thin housedress clung to her in spots where the wash water had splashed.

"How much is the bill down there now?" He asked.

"Seven dollars and twelve cents," Anna replied, sighing.

"I thought it was less than that. They took out four dollars from my last check, and the week before that, another two." He drummed his fingers nervously on the tabletop. He was beginning to despise the company store.

"I picked up a pair of shoes for Nellie last Wednesday. They were a dollar ten," she said. She searched his face for a reaction adding, "She starts school and she needs shoes."

"That company store might as well just own us," he said. He ran his scarred fingers through his hair in frustration.

"Well, tomorrow is payday, and I'll run them down five dollars," she said.

"Five?"

"Is that too much?"

"Better give them three," Harmon sighed heavily, "The rent is due this week."

Taking the job in the mine for McCoy Coal was something he did not want to do, but was forced to do. After the fire, the bank foreclosed on their land. They had no insurance and no way to pay for their loss. He tried to work out something with Mr. Holman, the bank president, but he was firm in his business. The bank owned the land now, and as luck would have it, they found six separate veins of rich black coal. Harmon had heard that the veins were three hundred feet thick in spots. He believed that the shareholders of the bank were getting rich by the minute.

He considered himself lucky though; after all, he had Anna and Nellie. They were the two things in his life that somehow kept him going into the earth and picking and shoveling coal cars full of the black gold for seventeen cents a carload. The job was aging him, however. Instead of feeling twenty-six, he felt more like fifty. The hours of crawling around on his hands and knees, sometimes in six inches of water with the roof of the mine only two inches away from his chest, would do that to a man.

Anna started supper, and he watched as she cut up the vegetables for the soup. Nellie played quietly out on the porch with a doll sewn out of old socks, giving it an almost human shape. The stitched red mouth of thread turned down at the side gave it a crooked smile. She loved it, even though she wished it had hair like hers: shiny, blonde, with big ringlets. It hung well below her shoulders.

"Time to eat," Anna said.

Nellie picked up the doll and walked into the kitchen. The smell of the fresh vegetable soup drifted through the house. Her father was already eating when she sat down and placed the doll next to her on the chair.

"Eat all of your soup and I'll give you something really good," Harmon said between bites.

"Peppermint?" She tilted her head quizzically to the side and picked up the spoon.

"Maybe," said Anna.

Harmon heard, but pretended to be oblivious to their conversation. On occasion he kept peppermint sticks in his lunch pail and every now and then he would bring one back for Nellie.

Nellie dug hungrily into the soup. She wondered if her doll would like a taste of the soup and what all this talk of school really meant. She hurriedly ate her supper thinking about the mysterious first day of school, and afterwards went to the living room with her father.

Nellie sat on Harmon's lap and savored the peppermint stick that he had given her. Anna was busy doing dishes in the kitchen.

"Are you going to school with me tomorrow?" Nellie asked him.

"No sweetheart, I have to work. Mommy is going to walk you down," he said.

Nellie bit off a piece of the peppermint stick and crunched it loudly. She looked in her father's eyes and asked softy, "When you went to school were you afraid?"

"No. You'll have lots of fun. I did," he said in a comforting tone as he wrapped his arms around her tiny shoulders.

Nellie finished the peppermint stick and slid from Harmon's lap. She looked at her father, who was now fast asleep on the chair. Gently tiptoeing across the floor, she went to the kitchen and watched as her mother poured the last of the water into the washtub.

After her bath, Nellie lay wide-eyed in her bed. It was still light outside and she fought the urge to sleep. The new dress hung on the back of her door and her new shoes were shined and ready on the top of the dresser. She stared and carefully counted the number of buttons on each shoe until she fell asleep.

* * *

Her mother's hand felt sweaty in hers as they walked down the wooden planked sidewalk toward the school. She clutched the small lard pail by the wire handle in her left hand. Inside the pail, fried potatoes were nestled between two slabs of cornbread and an apple. She felt curious, scared, and happy at the same time. She felt so big. She loved her new dress that Mama had sewn from the cloth flour sacks and had dyed a canary yellow. The carnation that her Daddy got her for the first day of school was pinned to her right breast. It was going into her flower book right after school, she thought, as she fingered the soft yellow pedals.

Her new shoes tapped on the wooden boards with each step. They drew closer to the school and her fingers gripped her mother's hand more tightly. The school stood in a large lot at the end of the row of company houses. It was on the same side of the main street as Nellie's house. They only had to go out the front door, to the left, and walk straight the quarter of a mile or so to the school. They were getting there much too quickly, she thought, feeling apprehensive as they passed the last house.

The wooden planks ended and a well-traveled dirt path cut through a grass covered lot and ended up on the front steps of the two-room schoolhouse. Nellie could see the brown brick building with the four windows facing the main street growing closer. The steps led up to a small wooden porch covered by a peaked roof. Her eyes loomed over the white double doors that were now opened wide and looking like a mouth ready to swallow her whole.

Kids were already running up the steps, laughing, and talking noisily as they disappeared inside the building. Nellie kept her head down, looking at her shoes as her right foot touched the first step. Petrified, it took great effort to put one foot in front of the other.

"Hello," a soothing voice magnetically caused her head to move upward from her shoes and look directly into the face of a middle-aged woman with wire-rimmed glasses and a gentle smile. It startled her and she felt herself tugging on her mother's hand, pulling her back automatically in the direction they had come.

"Why you must be Nellie, and I'd like to welcome you to your first day of school. I'm Mrs. Foster, your teacher." She stuck out her hand, extending it toward Nellie. The big people always shook hands, thought Nellie. She saw it many times down at the company store, and in the church on Sunday mornings. It was a big person thing to do. Slowly, she let go of her mother's hand, and reached out. The teacher's grip was gentle, and her hand felt soft.

"Come in, I'll show you the cloakroom and your desk."

Nellie released her grip from her mother.

"Listen to the teacher," Anna said. Hugging Nellie, one last time, she felt proud and sad as she turned and left.

"My desk? My very own desk?" Nellie asked the teacher as they walked through the door and into the cloakroom on the left.

"Yes. Right over there," pointing into the classroom where seven more first graders fidgeted in their seats. She helped Nellie with her sweater and hung it up on one of the black hooks screwed into the wall of the cloakroom. Mrs. Foster took the lunch pail from her hand and put it with the rest of them, on a shelf above the coats and sweaters. Nellie felt much better.

The morning went by quickly as the teacher tested each of the children. Nellie's mother had spent a lot of time reading and teaching her the alphabet at home, and it showed. Mrs. Foster thought she was a very bright child.

"Children?"

Eight faces looked up from their coloring. "It's time for lunch, so let's make a nice straight line, and I'll hand out your pails. If it's not done already, have your mothers scratch your names on your pails after school so I won't have to guess whose pail belongs to whom tomorrow."

Mrs. Foster stood on the porch of the schoolhouse and held up each tin pail. The children knew which one was theirs, except for two. She lifted the lids from the sand-bucket-sized pails and looked inside.

"Scrapple and biscuits," she said.

One of the two boys raised his hand. She handed the last lunch to the other. The boys ran off the porch to the side of the school where the others were already eating.

The girls stayed together and the boys ate in their group. There was no mingling, at that age, especially for the boys. The other side of the school was for the third grade students, who rarely bothered with the first and second graders. It seemed as if an invisible line divided the schoolyard. Far down in the yard were two wooden outhouses.

Nellie finished eating and her new friend, whose desk was behind hers, walked with her down to the privy. Nellie opened the door and went inside. It was hot and smelled, flies buzzed around, and she noticed a spider's web up in the top corner.

Nellie looked at the shafts of light shining through the cracks. The boards didn't quite fit together and, if she looked hard enough through the open cracks, she could see the other kids busy in the playground. She moved her face closer to the crack for a better look. An eyeball met hers. It was one of the third grade boys. She gasped and quickly jumped off the hole cut in the wooden seat. Hurriedly, she pulled up her cotton bloomers and smoothed down her dress. Outside, she looked around. Her friend had deserted her post.

She stomped over to three boys that were laughing. Her hands clamped her hips and she glared at the one who was laughing the hardest, the one in the red shirt. She had caught a glimpse of red through the crack of the outhouse when he ran.

"I'm telling the teacher," she said sharply.

"Go ahead."

Jimmy Holman, the bank president's son, cared little if she told. He smirked at her, and ran his fingers through his brown hair, plastered down on his head with hair cream and parted in the middle.

She was stunned as he stuck his freckled face right up to hers, nose to nose.

"You ain't nothin' but white trash, and that stupid lookin' posy on your dress don't make ya look any richer," he said.

She felt the misty spray of spit against her red-hot face. He lisped when he spoke. Her face burned and her mind blazed white as the tears came. The other kids had gathered around in a circle and watched the two of them. Nellie loosed a scream. She wanted to run away, or maybe just hit him in his freckled face so hard...that...that....

No one had ever talked to her that way before. She was sobbing uncontrollably by the time Mrs. Foster came marching down across the field and separated them.

She sat quietly in class until the first day of school ended. Her mother was waiting at the bottom of the steps to walk her home. Nellie walked in silence with her head down. At the path, Anna finally spoke up.

"How was it?"

"I hate it and I don't EVER want to go back."

"Why?" Anna said.

"A boy said I was white trash and made fun of my flower."

Her small hands clenched tight into balled fists.

Anna stopped and took her by the shoulders.

"Look at me."

Nellie looked up at her, pain painting her face. Anna put her finger under her chin and tilted her head up. Her big blue eyes were brimming with tears.

"You are not trash. Do you understand?" she said firmly, wiping the tears from her daughter's eyes. "Trash is something people throw away, and you are much too precious for that. The boy probably likes you and, sometimes, that is how little boys act to get your attention."

Nellie smiled weakly at the thought of that and sniffled. After all, he did try to peek into the outhouse. Maybe her mother was right. Maybe he did like her.

"Let's go home," Anna said. "Daddy will be home before long, and I have to start supper."

"Okay, Mom," she said.

The late afternoon sun of September felt warm on her back as they walked to the house. Her new friend, Bonnie Kay Jenkins, directed a wave to Nellie from across the dirt street, as she hurried in the opposite direction. Nellie waved back to her and yelled,

"See ya tomorrow."

Bonnie yelled something back, but Nellie could not hear her over the sound of the horse drawn ice wagon rattling its way up the dirt street.

When she got home, she took the carnation off her dress and pressed it into the book that her Mother had made for her. Anna wrote on the bottom of the page: "My first day of school. September 6, 1905." Anna guided Nellie's hand as she helped her write her name under the date.

FOUR
FUNERALS AND FLOWERS

"Daddy, Daddy, look. Look, my report card."

Waving the card in the air, Nellie could not wait for him to step into the kitchen and she rushed toward him. "I passed," she said. He moved and she followed.

"Lookie—right here." She pointed her finger to the bottom of the report card. "Exported to the second grade," she shouted and squealed with delight.

"Don't you mean, promoted?" Harmon said, as he stepped inside and plucked the report card from her raised hand.

"Yeah, I guess," she repeated, "Prooo—moted." She repeated the long O sound, just to make sure she had it right this time.

"I got one smart girl here, don't I, Anna?"

"You sure do." Anna dried her wet hands on a towel and put the last glass up in the white cupboard above the sink.

"Guess what else?" Nellie asked Harmon, as she stood looking up at him with one hand on her hip.

"I dunno." He bent down to pull of his boot, "What?"

"Jimmy Holman has to do third grade all over again, and boy was his Daddy mad." She swiped the air with her little hand. "He whupped him all the way up to their house."

Harmon looked over at Anna, a smile on his coal-smudged face. "Every dog has its day." She laughed and threw the hand towel at him.

School had been out for more than a month, and the mid-July sun blazed down on the entire town. It was still and quiet, a time of barely rustling leaves that drooped with surrender to the attacking heat of the day.

Nellie played in the backyard in her bare feet; the high button school shoes and buttonhook were no longer required. The grass felt cool and tickled the bottoms of her feet as she walked to the end of the yard. A board fence ran the entire length of the row of houses. It was unpainted and rough to her touch. The fence was too high for her to climb. She had tried before, so she just looked for a knothole.

Finding an eye-sized hole, she swept away the spider webs and splinters with her fingers. Putting her face against the fence, centering her eye on the hole until she could see clearly, she watched. The creek ran cool behind the fence and she heard some kids splashing and laughing. She could see boys through the hole and thought of sneaking out of the yard and around the fence.

They sure look like they are having fun, she thought. She moved her eyeball to the left and back to the right. Her eye focused on the big tree on the left and scanned to the gray boulder halfway out in the middle of the creek. One of the boys moved too far to the right of the boulder and out of her view. The other two splashed water on each other. She struggled to hear what they were saying. They were laughing and scooping up pieces of wet clay. When it landed on their tanned backs and stomachs, it stuck to them and looked to her like they had big freckles.

She continued looking through the knothole, stopping and moving her face from the hole every few minutes to rest. She leaned forward with both hands on the fence and bent at the waist resting her watery eye. Spying is hard work, she thought.

"Skinny dipping time," one of the boys yelled. She put her eye back to the hole. The way the boy said it, it had to be something very special, she thought. The two boys were still in the middle of the creek flinging mud and slapping water at each other.

"I wonder what skinny dipping means," she whispered. She peered harder, when the boy who had disappeared earlier suddenly came into sight, buck-naked.

She gasped, but didn't move her eye from the hole. She never saw anything like it. She felt devilish, like she shouldn't be doing it, but she was mesmerized. The boy was different from her. She wondered if that thing between his legs was his pee hole, and why did it look so darn different from hers?

The boy jumped into the creek, his feet and legs making splashing sounds amidst the laughter of the other two. Nellie giggled, and put her hand up to cover her mouth. Suddenly, she remembered the voice. Yep, sure enough, it was Jimmy Holman. She took one last look and turned away from the fence, feeling vindicated.

"Every dog has its tray," she muttered to herself, "or something like that." She marched up to the house, head held high and feeling very smug about getting even for the outhouse incident at school.

"Hi Mama," she said, hoping that her voice didn't give away what she just witnessed. She probably knows, she thought: Mothers know everything. Nellie studied her for some sign of magic intuition. Anna busily patched a pair of Harmon's pants.

"Hi, baby," she replied concentrating on the pants.

She pulled the needle through the patch and up into the air. Nellie almost wanted to tell her. Maybe it would make her seem bigger to her mother if she knew, as if she had graduated to a higher level in life or something. It suddenly occurred to her she might not be allowed in the back yard again. She decided not to say anything.

Anna looked up at her. Their eyes met, and Nellie felt her throat going dry in an instant. Her mother's gaze went past her eyes and shifted over her head to the clock on the shelf behind her. "It's almost time for your daddy to come home. Are you going to hide behind the door?"

Nellie exhaled, "Uh, yeah...sure." She darted out of the living room into the kitchen, trembling with relief. She slid behind the door and crouched, her knees just beginning to feel normal again. The uneasy feeling in her stomach from almost having to be untruthful slowly subsided.

Nellie waited behind the door. The boots were scraping on the wooden planks, getting closer. She looked through the crack of the inside door. He was almost there. She loved this game, and wondered what her Daddy would do this time when she scared him. The soles thumped oddly across the porch. She held her breath, waiting. This time she thought, she would stay crouched down, wrapping her arms around his legs when he stepped inside. Maybe roar like a lion or a wild tiger, she imagined.

Three hammering knocks shook the wooden frame of the screen door. It startled her and she looked through the crack. Two men stood at the door. Men she never saw before. The biggest one cleared his throat. Nellie got up from behind the wooden door and stood on the inside of the screen door, facing them.

"Hello, sweetheart," the big man said, "Is your Momma home?" The shorter man's eyes were red and watering. Anna had heard the knock from the other room and was already in the doorway that separated the kitchen from the living room. She walked up to the door and gently moved Nellie to the side, placing a hand on the top of her head.

"Mrs. Bell?" The big man inquired. She noticed that the shorter one had trouble keeping eye contact.

"Yes."

"My name's Dan McCoy, I own the coalmine." He seemed nervous to her.

"Would you mind coming out on the porch, I hate to talk in front of your little girl."

"Stay here honey, I'll be right back."

Nellie sensed something and she quite didn't know what to make of it. Her mother walked out onto the porch, closing the big inside door. It occurred to her that it was much too hot in the house to close that big old door. No one in any of the company houses shut them, not even at night, and definitely not in the middle of July. Nellie heard the big man talking.

Along with the muffled talk, Nellie thought she heard her mother crying, and listened harder. She picked out some of the words the man said, gas, and not sure, and, there still could be some hope. They talked for a long time, and she heard their boots scrape across the porch, then down the wooden steps.

She watched the doorknob turn, and her mother pushing the door with her right elbow very slow until it stopped against the wall. She was holding the pants that she had been patching, her hands wringing them as if she just washed them.

"Mama?" Nellie said, softly.

"Oh, baby, baby," she whispered, closing her eyes. Tears rolled down her cheeks.

"What, Mama. What?" Nellie tugged at Anna's dress, just as her mother dropped the pants on the kitchen floor and lifted her up into her arms. She felt her mother's breasts heaving against her cheeks with each sob and the tears felt wet and hot on the back of her neck.

Her Mama told her about her Daddy. She still didn't understand it. Her Mama kept saying, "all we can do is pray". Nellie ate by herself that night and kept watching and listening for her Daddy.

Later, in her mother's bed, she dozed off. She woke up sometime during the night to find her Mama was sleeping close beside her. It was also the first time in her life that Daddy was not with them. Nothing made sense; she only slept in the bed with them a few times when she used to be afraid of the thunderstorms.

The cool air blew in through the window in waves and felt good against her hot and sticky skin. She was lying on her back, with her hands behind her neck, and her left leg crossed over the right one. She could feel the mattress move, ever so slightly, each time her Mama exhaled and inhaled.

The room was black and, in the darkness, she sensed she was staring at the ceiling. She moved her right hand from behind her neck and extended her forefinger slowly moving it toward her face just to see if she could see it, and to double check if her eyes were as wide open as they felt like they were. Her fingertip brushed against her eyelash and she jerked. She was still awake, she thought to herself.

"I miss you Daddy, and I wish you were here," she whispered in the dark.

"If you come back I promise I'll never look through the hole in the fence at Jimmy Holman's pee hole." She thought God was punishing her this way for looking through the fence. At last, she fell asleep.

In the morning, some of the men who worked with her Daddy helped to move the furniture out of the living room. They all seemed nice to her, one of them even gave her a nickel. They put the furniture out on the back porch and left the big couch and the pictures on the wall. She watched as four of them brought in a long black table and set it up against the wall, covering it with a silky blue cloth.

She never saw so many flowers at one time. They were all brought in and arranged to the right and left of the big table. When no one was looking, she took one of the red roses and sneaked back to her room with it. She opened the book and gingerly put the rose in the center of the page. The thick pencil felt comfortable in between her fingers. She could print now. Her report card said so: one hundred percent in the penmanship box.

Sitting cross-legged on the floor, concentrating, the tip of her tongue sticking out through her teeth as she bit down, she printed in her best block letters. Looking at the finished writing, she quickly nodded her head in approval. The sentence went downhill a bit and she spelled with the phonetic mind of a six year old, "My Daddy's Fewnneral, Juli 27,1907."

FIVE
MOTHERS DAY

In the recreational room at Beacon Manor, the lady flipping the letters on the game show on television smiled. It reminded Nellie of a game she used to play as a kid. Hangman was the name, if she remembered correctly. The woman flipping the letters over on the big board had her hair pinned up on the top of her head, and Nellie admired the style. Once, she had worn her hair in a similar fashion.

Nellie looked around at the other residents. The lady with her hair yanked out sat in her wheelchair, her head cocked insanely to the side, her frail body leaning to the right. If it hadn't been for the strap tied around her waist and through the back of the wheel chair, Nellie thought, surely the old woman would roll right out on to the floor. The woman weakly tugged and picked at the strap. She talked quietly to herself.

"I'd like to buy a vowel," blared from the floor model television turned up loud for the benefit of the hard of hearing. It hurt Nellie's ears.

Three patients sat in a line on the brown leather couch: a bald headed man, a rotund woman, and Gertie, the teacher. The bald man's left suspender dangled from his left shoulder. Transfixed to the television, he wasn't aware that it had become unsnapped.

The rather large woman was in her sixties, Nellie guessed. Her hair stuck out in all directions. It was a mousy brown with streaks of gray in it. She sat to the bald man's left. Her hot pink housedress was

34

tent sized and drooped between her fat, open legs. Gertie sat on the right of the man, protectively clutching a yellow note pad. She scribbled furiously with each correct choice of letter. Nellie noticed that Gertie's silver specked, tortoiseshell, horn-rimmed glasses were just about to slide off her narrow nose.

Nellie watched closely when Mr. Banks shuffled onto the brown carpet that designated the thirty square foot area known as the "Patient's Lounge." He turned his long, thin, hollow cheeked face slowly, searching from patient to patient. His silver hair, cut in a crew cut, bristled with the help of some kind of hair cream. Nellie thought it looked like an upside down hairbrush.

He stood there, his back slightly stooped with his left hand in his pocket, reducing his six-foot frame by an inch or two. In his right hand was an aluminum cane with a small, white rubber cap at the bottom. He wore a dark, long sleeved green shirt buttoned up the front. The shirt hung over his thin frame. It looked too big on him. His plain blue pants were hiked up over his stomach, closer to his chest than his waist, and the end of his black belt overlapped so far that it hung through a belt loop and drooped down a good three inches in front of his pants. The leather flapped against his pant leg when he walked.

Banks looked over at Nellie sitting in the maroon cloth recliner, a coffee table dividing her from another empty, padded wooden rocking chair. She concentrated on the television, hoping he wouldn't notice her. She pretended to be studying it hard, hoping he would just go away, or maybe have a seat in the other empty recliner by the couch.

"Is there an L?" The young man from Elmira, New York, said on the television, just as Nellie caught Banks eyeing her up.

"Oh brother, just what I need today," she muttered.

She didn't want to be bothered today with his nonsense. In fact, her growing disgust with the place made her more anxious than ever to leave.

He walked over to her, shuffling slowly in front of her, blocking her view. His cane bumped the coffee table with a metallic click. He grabbed onto the arm of the chair, turned, and sank down, his arms stretched out on the chair's curved cherry wood arms. His wrinkled hands wrapped around them and he began to rock.

"Well, Miss Bell. Is all well?" Banks said, slowly enunciating each word, in a soft cracking voice. A devilishly teasing grin escaped, showing his snuff-stained teeth.

She hated his little rhyme. When he wasn't talking to her in poor French, he would make up these silly little rhymes using her name, and she was growing impatient with him. She ignored him and looked at the TV. The game show was over and replaced by another. Nellie had to think of a way to get out of here. She might be seventy-four, but she was sharp. Sure, she was a little slow physically, but her mind seemed to grow more alert. She just did not belong here. She reaffirmed that continuously in her mind.

"World cities for three hundred," said the homemaker from Bethlehem, Pennsylvania, who hoped to be a writer someday.

Nellie busied herself thinking of a way to escape this madness. She loved her freedom. She had been that way all of her life and being here was eating her up, mind and soul. She didn't care if she walked out of here or if they carried her out. One way or another, she would leave. A smell drifted across the open space of the lobby and she covered her nose with her hand, still looking at the television. The yanked out hair woman had lost control in her pants.

"What is Paris?" the homemaker replied in the form of a question to the applause of the studio audience.

Gordon Banks rocked madly in the chair, yelling at the top of his lungs, "Viva La France, Viva La France." His feet were nearly coming of the floor.

"Nurse, Nurse!" the lady with the soiled pants screamed, her head still cocked to the side.

"To the principal's office, young man," yelled Mrs. Martz, pointing a shaky finger across the way at Mr. Banks. Nellie grasped her walker with both hands, pulled herself up from the recliner, and walked back to her room. On the walk back, the smell of human waste and pine scented cleaner hung in the stagnant hot air of the hallway, and she became even more determined to escape this madness.

* * *

Later that evening, Elaina walked into the room carrying a plastic supper tray with both hands. She set the tray on the top of the dresser and stepped out into the hallway, returning with a small stand with folded metal legs. Moving Nellie's walker from the front of the chair, she opened the tray, putting it within reach of her. With everything set, she picked up the supper tray and placed it on the stand.

"Well, is it Filet Mignon and lobster?" Nellie asked. They both laughed.

"That's on Tuesdays," Elaina played along with her. She enjoyed Nellie's sense of humor.

"Nope, tonight it's tomato soup and grilled cheese, madam," Elaina said, faking an accent and lowering her voice, like an English butler. She lifted the plastic lid off the tray with a dramatic sweep of her hand.

"I was worried about you, Nellie," Elaina said, "Why didn't you come to the dining room?" Elaina was also concerned about Nellie depending on the walker, but said nothing about it.

She walked over to the dresser and put the plastic lid on top of it, turned, and sat on the corner of the bed with her hands folded across her lap.

Nellie looked at her, this black woman with her hair braided and dangling down to the shoulders of her white uniform top, and then she answered, "Because they make me sick." She looked directly into the almond, shaped black eyes of the attractive, twenty six year old woman, without blinking an eyelash.

"They're bad off, Miss Nellie. They don't mean any harm by it. They don't even understand what they're doing most of the time." Elaina's soft, soothing voice musically twanged with a slight, deep Southern accent.

"I know that, but it grates on my nerves. I feel like I'm the only normal one in here most of the time. I wished I'd never fallen down those steps and broke my hip. That's what started it all. Plus, my daughter's motives weren't the most honorable either."

Elaina knew about Nellie's daughter, Barbara, from the many talks the two of them had over the last eighteen months. Nellie told her just about everything having to do with her. The last time Elaina saw her was on Mother's Day, a year ago. Elaina sensed a wickedness and greediness about her that really turned her off. She had an unusual air about her. Elaina remembered her being arrogant, haughty, and fake. Very fake.

"Well, guess what?" Elaina said, shifting on the edge of the bed.
"What?"

"Tomorrow is Mother's Day, and your daughter called. She's coming down from Dallas and bringing her husband with her. She said to tell you to be ready, because they're taking you out for lunch." Elaina smiled broadly, showing her straight, white teeth, surrounded by perfect full lips.

"Oh joy," Nellie said sarcastically, plopping her half-eaten grilled cheese sandwich down on her plate. "It'll probably be my treat. That tub of lard husband of hers is tighter than wet leather."

Elaina laughed loud and said, "Now Miss Bell, be nice." She glanced at her watch and jumped off the bed.

"I have to go now; I didn't realize I was here this long. I'll see you when I am back here. I'm off the next two days. Someone will be by to pick up your tray later." She walked to the door and turned around, "Be good, sweetie, and don't be too hard on your son-in-law." She sang her words teasingly, and wagged her finger at her when she said son-in-law. She winked at Nellie and laughed. Nellie picked up the grilled cheese sandwich and feigned throwing it at her. She quickly ducked out the door. Nellie heard her whistling loudly down the hallway.

Nellie took a bite of the soup and set the spoon down. She didn't have much of an appetite: She hadn't since she was wheeled into this place. It was only going to be "temporary", her daughter once told her. When her hip healed and the therapy was over, she would be going home. She should have known better to trust Barbara, she thought.

The nurse with the meds appeared, rolling the cart through her doorway. Nellie turned from the window and watched her as she went through the mechanics of looking at the clipboard, picking up the cup with the two blue sleeping pills in it, handing it to her, and then turning to get the plastic pitcher of water from underneath the cart.

Nellie looked at the two pills in the bottom of the cup, and back at the nurse still bending over and looking in the bottom of the cart. Nellie was nervous, expecting her to turn at any second, catching her, and foiling her plan. Keeping her eyes steadily on her, Nellie slid the two pills between the cushion and arm of the chair. She knew if they ever found out, they would watch her like a hawk from now on and check her mouth, under her tongue, anything to make sure she took the damn things.

Nellie performed the cup exchange with closed eyes. She tilted back her head, and put the cup to her lips and drank. She shook her head and shoulders in one quick shuddering motion, as a child taking castor oil would, and then looked at the nurse.

"Blah. I hate those things," she said.

"Good girl, Nellie," the nurse praised her in a tone intended for a young child.

"Would you hand me my flower book off the top of my dressing drawer before you leave?" Nellie asked as the nurse checked her chart.

"Sure." She walked over to the fiberboard chest and picked up the book, looking admiringly at the lacy border.

"Here you go, sweetie," she put the book in Nellie's outstretched hands.

"Thank you so much," Nellie said, over dramatizing the sweetness in her voice, keeping the nurse off guard by hiding the fear she felt for sticking the pills down in the chair.

"Well, I've got a lot of work to do. Good night, Nellie," the nurse said as she pushed the cart to the door.

"Good night."

Her ribs hurt as she took a deep breath and exhaled. Her depression was deep, and the desperation to leave this place grew with each dreadful passing minute.

Flipping the book over and looking at the cloth covering the heavy paper backing, she turned it locating the old pink embroidery thread tied in a knot and pushed underneath. Concentrating on the lower left-hand corner of the book's spine and using her thumbnail, she picked at the cover until it lifted up from the old yellow mucilage glue that held the cloth to the thick paper cover. Sliding the embroidery thread out, it dangled down and left enough of a space so that by sliding her sharp thumbnail back and forth, she created a two-inch pocket.

Reaching down with her left hand, she searched blindly between the arm and cushion until she felt the two little pills. Pinching them between her thumb and finger, she slowly and gingerly slid her hand out of the tight space. Laying them on the last page of the book and looking at them, she wondered how many it would take. She slid the pills into the pocket she created, and smoothed down the cloth. With the book closed, the three-inch piece of pink thread with the knot at the end dangled down like a bookmark.

She slept peacefully that night, comfortable with her decision and content to know that she would soon be out of this dreaded place. She rose early in the morning, bathed, and dressed. She sat in her chair waiting for her daughter. The nursing home was bustling with families coming and going, some guilty over the fact that they came only once a year; others more bored and wishing they were somewhere else.

Nellie looked out the window watching the May sun beat down on the green grass that flowed out and stopped at the concrete curbing separating the yard from the parking lot. The crape myrtles bloomed now, and the pink flowers hung heavily all over the trees. She watched two fat robins flitting and chirping loudly at each other. The parking lot was nearly full with all the visitor's cars and she studied each one looking for the silver Cadillac Fleetwood that her daughter drove. Probably bought with the money they got from selling her house, she thought.

She waited and watched until the parking lot was nearly empty. She watched the families get in their cars and leave, and watched as the sun was showing only halfway behind the line of the horizon and the sky. The last car pulled out of the lot and turned left, its red taillight blinking to signal the turn with someone waving from the back seat.

Leaving her walker by the chair, she walked to the dresser and pulled open the drawer. Sliding the gold bracelet off her wrist, she dropped it into the wooden jewelry box. Reaching over, she closed the door to her room.

She took the blue dress off that she had picked for the occasion, hung it in the closet, and put on her blue housecoat. Crawling into bed, she propped herself up with a pillow against the headboard and opened the book to where she had left off. Dried mistletoe taped to the page with three strips of yellowed cellophane tape, together with the looping letters of a happy teenager, stared up at her with the words, "Merry Christmas 1916."

SIX
MISTLETOE AND MOONSTONE

Seventeen-year-old Cotton Pearce parked the Model T and slammed the door with a metallic thud. He fumbled with the slide lock on the wrought iron gate leading up the snow-shoveled sidewalk to the two-story red brick house. The portico's four columns glowed a faint white from the electric lights reflecting from inside. The iron railing on the flat deck roof of the portico glistened with a thin coating of ice. He pounded on the heavy wooden door six times. His knuckles were ready to rap on it again when it swung open.

"Cotton Pearce, it does take a certain amount of time to get to the door. You're always in such a big hurry," Nellie said, standing in the doorway. "You might as well come in out of the cold," she said looking down at the canvas bag dangling from his left hand.

"Where's your Mama?" he said, his eyes nervously looking at his feet and then to her.

"Suppose you have some more squirrels for her," Nellie said, with a just enough sweet disgust in her voice to make him stammer.

"Uh, uh, yeah, as a matter of fact, I do." He shifted his weight from one booted foot to the other.

"Mother," Nellie yelled in the direction of the kitchen, "you want some squirrels?" She looked at Cotton with her blue eyes and turned her nose up slightly. "I hope you cleaned them this time," she whispered loud enough for only him to hear and with a measured sarcasm that made the tips of his ears turn red.

"How many do you have?" Anna walked into the large room from the kitchen, her apron coated with flour, and a wooden rolling pin in her hand.

"I got twelve, ma'am. And there ain't a one of them been shot anywhere but in the head," he said proudly, looking at Nellie for some sign of approval. She rolled her eyes.

"Plenty of good meat on 'em," he added.

"Well, young man, why don't you bring them out to the kitchen and I'll take a look at them. I just made some hot cocoa and you look like you're mighty cold."

"Real cold ma'am," Cotton said. He appreciated her offer, but did his best to hide the excitement on his thin, young face.

Anna smiled, noticing the boy's nervousness.

"Come on," she said.

He followed her into the kitchen, leaving a wet trail of melted snow on the hardwood floors. Nellie looked at the floor and shook her head wide-mouthed with disbelief as she watched the gangly, blonde haired young man disappear into the kitchen across her newly polished floor. She stomped her right foot and crossed her arms, tapping the toe of her right shoe on the floor.

"Men," she said, whispering through her clenched teeth.

Eight years had passed since Harmon's death in the mine. With the onetime death benefit paid by the coal company and a small life insurance policy, they had managed to survive. Anna purchased the ten-room house on the west side of Oak Hill and opened up her door to boarders. There were plenty.

With the town growing and the railroad going through, opportunities unloaded at the gray clapboard train station daily. The boarding house's location was just across the tracks and advertised cheap rates. The stationmaster was fond of Anna's fried chicken and often sent business her way. Immigrants, without the knowledge of English, simply nodded with wide smiles when he pointed to the big house and rubbed his stomach.

The growing number of merchants in town each plucked some amount from the pay envelopes of the miners. Every thirteen days, the town bustled with men, women, and children from towns with names like Whipple, Scarboro, and Summerlee. Two new movie theaters were crammed full of people on the weekends, and vendors hawked their wares on sidewalk space worth fighting over.

"Some man's sellin' Christmas trees down in front o' the company store," Cotton said, licking the cocoa from his upper lip, "Forty cents for one. A half dollar if you git it with the tinsel."

Anna shook her head.

"I can't believe they're selling trees nowadays. Harmon and I used to climb up to Coal Ridge with a saw and drag the thing all the way back down to the house. That was the fun of it. Picking one out and slipping and sliding back down off that hill," Anna said fondly.

"Mama, can we get one?" asked Nellie. Her blue eyes danced with excitement.

"I don't see any reason we can't have a tree. Christmas will be here day after tomorrow, and as long as we keep it watered, it should be okay. "

Anna paused, thinking how to get the tree from the town to the boarding house.

"It's a long walk to the company store," she said.

"I have my Dad's flivver parked right outside, I kin take Nellie," Cotton said quickly.

"Mama, I finished my chores and my schoolwork's done," Nellie said.

Realizing she might have given Cotton the impression of being interested, she added,

"I mean, I guess I could go down, just to look. That is unless you need me to help serve the boarders."

Anna dug into her apron pocket, a small cloud of flour dust rose from the apron as she searched. She pulled out a half dollar and slid it across the kitchen table toward Nellie.

"I want a nice one now, you hear," Anna said.

Cotton leapt from the table and hurried to the front door. Nellie made him wait as she deliberately took her time getting her coat.

Anna met them at the door and held out a dyed wool scarf.

"You better take this," she said. Nellie slid it around her thin neck. Anna looked at the two of them.

Cotton was tall and looked awkward with his black and red plaid wool coat hanging off his shoulders. His blue hat, with the ear flaps pulled down, left his light blonde, almost cotton-colored hair, wisping out in curls from underneath it.

Her little girl had grown, it seemed, much too quickly. She was a beautiful young woman now. Nellie's long blond hair hung well past the middle of her back, the ends dark with the soft brown color of a ripe pecan. Her pouting lips were full, and her blue eyes had long lashes that curled upward to her naturally arched eyebrows. She had her mother's nose, upturned, giving her an air of natural dignity.

Nellie opened the door and Cotton stepped out. She reached out quickly and grabbed him by the elbow of his wool coat, stopping him before his other leg crossed the threshold. He turned with a puzzled look on his face.

With a firm Southern drawl, Nellie said, "I do swear Cotton Pearce…where did you get your manners from anyway?"

Red-faced, he stepped back allowing her to go ahead of him. He glanced at Anna and shrugged. Anna smiled, watching him plod behind Nellie in the December snowfall.

Back in the kitchen, Anna pumped water from the top of the wooden sink. The hand pump, attached to the top of the sink, screeched and clunked. The bottom of the bucket dripped cold droplets on the griddles of the hot iron stove, filling the room with sizzling hisses as she set it down. A bucket behind it boiled and, with a rag around her hand, she lifted it off by the wire handle.

The mudroom behind the kitchen door provided a place to hang clothes in the cold winters, as well as privacy for the boarders to bathe. A cloud of steam rose from the galvanized tub as she poured the last bucket of water. She took a towel from a wooden shelf and hung it on a nail poking out from the dark green wall. With a soft plop, she dropped a bar of lye soap into the water.

"Frankie, your bath is ready."

"Coming," a voice answered with a thick, Hungarian accent. A man appeared in the doorway, balancing on the hump of the threshold in his worn work boots. His size nearly blocked the kitchen light outlining his broad shoulders. He was olive skinned with coal black curly hair, and a big handlebar mustache. She noticed gentleness in his soft brown eyes. Anna handed him a wooden handled scrub brush and closed the door on her way to the kitchen.

* * *

Cotton wheeled the car into the snow-covered lot at the side of the company store. He jumped out and opened Nellie's door. She smiled at him, satisfied that she managed to teach him some kind of etiquette. They walked past the front of the white washed building to the other side, where a string of bulbs cordoned off a lot full of trees. The White Pines, Scotch, and Douglas fir trees in long lines leaned on crossed boards nailed to the sawed off trunks. Pine scent filled her nostrils and she breathed deep.

Nellie walked through the row of trees with Cotton close at her heels. She checked branches and shook them like a campaigning politician begging for votes. She glad-handed her way down through the rows of trees as snowflakes tickled her face.

Cotton eyed her every move. He had a warm feeling, a glowing that radiated through his body making his heart feel wrapped in spun sugar. The lids of his eyes grew heavy with daydreams of him and her.

She pointed to a huge pine that stood out with great height over the others.

"I like this one."

Cotton's head bent back as if he was looking at the sky when his eyes moved up the trunk. He shook his head and shrugged.

He crouched down ,wrapped his hands around the thick trunk of the tree, and slid it out until it toppled over in the snow. He held onto the crossed wood nailed to the bottom and dragged it toward a man standing by a roaring fire barrel. The width of the bushy branches forced other couples to part to let him pass.

The man at the barrel rubbed his chin as he sized up the tree.

"That's a dollar tree you have there, son."

"A dollar?" Cotton asked surprised. "Sign says forty and fifty cents."

"Sorry son, but that's a mighty nice tree, it's bigger than the rest and it's a Douglas fir to boot. It had to be brought down all the way from Canada."

Nellie reached into her pocket and held out the fifty-cent piece. Cotton fumbled around in the pocket of his wool coat pulling out a silver dollar he had managed to hide away for more than a year. His fingers were slow to release the treasured coin.

"Merry Christmas," he said, with a broad grin. He folded her fingers around the coin in her hand until it was out of sight in her clenched fist. The man threw in enough rope to tie the tree to the Model T's roof. On the way to the car, Nellie thought better of Cotton Pearce, even if he could stand to learn some manners.

Nellie and Cotton returned home with the tree. The well-fed boarders who had been reading newspapers in the parlor met them. They all helped push and pull the monstrosity through the doors, across the dining room, and into the parlor. After standing it up in the corner near the fireplace, the treetop nearly touched the tall ceiling.

"Everyone, please, please take a seat," Anna said. "I'll be right back." Two of the boarders sat on the wicker settee: the fellow from Wales, and the young mining engineer from Chicago. Frankie stood by the crackling fireplace, his elbow resting on the oak mantle. The last two, an Irishman they called Paddy, and Carlos, an Italian, each pulled up a wingback wicker chair that matched the settee. They sat with their backs to the tree, facing the others. Nellie sat on the red and gold rug carpeting the floor. Cotton stood at the big bay window. The talk of the men turned to the war in Europe.

They conversed of faraway places and Cotton listened intently while watching the heavy snow falling outside. Places like France, Germany, and names like Huns and the Kaiser reached his ears. He had heard the men in town talking about the United States getting involved in a "conflict". They were mostly older men down at the Ford filling station doing the talking, and they were the ones who fought in the Civil War, still believing that the North could have been beaten.

Cotton imagined he was picking off Huns, like the squirrels he brought to Anna. He imagined that the Huns probably sported big mustaches like Frankie's that curled silver like the tails of the squirrels. He saw them falling out of the trees, some of them hanging on with one hand, just before they dropped to the ground. He was just starting to think about a big parade honoring him with President Wilson riding beside him when Anna came back into the room.

"Who would like a nice hot cup of spiced cider?" she asked. She held a tray with cups and a copper teakettle. Nellie rose from the floor and helped pour the steaming drink into each cup. They served the boarders with flowing movements and charm.

When Anna reached Cotton, he said, "I can't. I gotta get back home. Thanks just the same Mrs. Bell," He walked across the room nodding to each of the boarders.

"Wait," Nellie said, setting her cup on the low wooden coffee table in front of the settee. "I'll see you to the door." She followed him out of the parlor and to the door leading to the porch.

She looked at him with searching eyes.

"Thanks for the tree. Can you come by tomorrow night?" she asked.

"Mebbe," Cotton said. He looked at the floor and stammered, "I gotta go."

Nellie lifted the curtain and peeked through the window, watching as he walked to the car.

* * *

By mid-morning, Anna finished baking the last of the cookies and set plates of them around the house, along with lit candles. She still followed her Swedish traditions. The candles would stay lit and the cookies were for guests. Frankie would be staying. Her sister, Phyllis, and her husband should be arriving from Charleston on the five o' clock train. She wanted to make tonight a special Christmas Eve.

Anna stirred the rice pudding, folding the mixture repeatedly. Risgrynsaksak was the Swedish name for it. She wished she had some lingonberries to cover the top of the creamy mixture. Lifting the wooden spoon from the pudding, she tasted it, and then reached into her apron pocket and pulled out a small silver ring. Holding it over the mixture, she watched it land on top and then disappear with her stirring. According to tradition, if an unmarried person found it they would be married within the year. If a married person found the ring, no weddings would come to the house in the following year.

Anna lifted the heavy porcelain bowl and moved it to join the pies and breads, filling the counter top of the larder. The wooden kitchen table was loaded with cranberry relish and loaves of fruitcake. The smell of the goose, stuffed with apples and raisins, roasted in the oven of the cook stove, filling the house with a mouth-watering aroma. She slid out a chair and sat down to rest before the company arrived.

The newspaper on the table caught her attention and she picked it up. News about the war over in Europe was the front-page story. She feared that the United States would become involved in it. The talk about it being a World War sent a shiver of fear through her. She hoped nothing would come of it, and it would end before any men would have to leave West Virginia to fight, like her uncle had that died in the Spanish American War.

In the parlor, Nellie finished the last paper chain and draped it around the branches of the tree. She called for Anna with excitement and pride in her voice.

"Mama, come see."

Anna stood with her hands on her hips, admiring the tree. Popcorn strings and paper chains decorated the thick branches of the massive tree. Silver, red and gold glass ornaments hung throughout it. The tree looked beautiful, she thought.

"It's so pretty. You did such a good job," Anna said, giving Nellie a hug.

"Did you invite Cotton to the Christmas Eve dinner?" Anna asked.

"Yes, Mama, I did. I hope he can make it. He's sort of shy."

"Well, there's something under the tree for him. I hope he likes it. After all, he did bring a lot of game here this last year. It sure helped cut the cost of feeding the boarders. He never takes a penny for it either." She took Nellie's hand in hers, looked at her and added, "I think he's a real nice boy, too."

Nellie was not seeking her mother's approval; after all, she would not turn sixteen until April, the rightful age for courting in this part of the country. It made her feel good that her mother liked him; however, she had not looked at Cotton as a serious suitor.

"Do I get to pin my hair up now, Mama?" Nellie asked nervously.

Anna looked at her and thought of how she had asked her own mother the same thing after she met Harmon. Pinning up her hair advertised a coming of age. It was a moment Nellie, and any girls her age, anxiously waited for around all of West Virginia.

"Nellie, I wish your father was here to help me sometimes. I know he would be very proud of you, and I think he would have liked Cotton."

Anna thought about this step into womanhood; a sad reminder that one day, Nellie would be gone and on her own.

"I'll help you pin it. I have your Grandmother's hairpin in my jewelry box. Come on."

In Anna's bedroom, an excited Nellie admired her new look in the big mirror. Anna felt this step was just one of many that would lead her to independence and someday away from home. She covered the undeniable thought with a weak smile.

* * *

The five o'clock passenger train was running late due to the snow. Anna stood inside the station, warmed by the pot-bellied stove in the waiting area. A few people milled about, glancing at their watches impatiently. Nellie sat on the long wooden bench, her blonde hair up and a cameo brooch choker around her thin neck. She tucked her hands in a fur muffler. Cotton walked over and held out a bag of roasted peanuts, putting them just under her nose. "Want some?" he asked.

"Sure," Nellie said, sliding her hands out of the muffler and digging into the little cloth bag. They warmed her hands, and she clenched them for a moment, enjoying the heat.

"Snowin' hard now," Cotton said. His eyes stared out the big window, giving him a view of the wooden porch and the two sets of tracks that ran parallel to the building. He cracked open another peanut and popped it in his mouth, tossing the broken shells into a bucket at the end of the bench.

"Here it comes," some woman said, towing a small black haired boy about four years old on her skirt tails. With her announcement, every head in the place turned to the window. A white headed black porter, his saucer cap cocked to the side, opened the door, and the train's shrill whistle shook the building. The hissing steam clouded the view of the train for a moment until the wind pushed it down the tracks. The anxious group shuffled outside as the passengers walked off the train. The passengers clung to their hats and coats, fighting an insistent wind.

"There they are," Anna said, waving her hand in the air, "Over here."

A man and woman made their way to the platform. The woman rushed to Anna and they embraced. It was the first time she had seen her sister in years.

Back at Anna's, six people gathered around, watching, as Anna put the bowl of pudding on the table. Taking a seat she said, "I hope you all enjoy this. I couldn't find lingonberries so I covered it with some blueberries that I canned last fall."

"I haven't had this since we were kids back at home," Phyllis said, picking up her spoon and dipping it into the pudding. She winked at Nellie since she knew the tradition. The clinking spoons were briefly interrupted when Phyllis said, "Nellie, they opened a new school for secretaries in Charleston. Have you taken any typing in school?"

"Yes ma'am, I am taking it now," Nellie answered.

"Have you given any thought to going on after you graduate," Phyllis said, looking from Nellie to her mother.

"I have a few articles that I looked at."

"Well, it's going to be one of the best schools in the country, so I hear."

"What the..." Frankie put his hand up to his mouth and, embarrassed, pulled out a silver ring, holding up it toward the light and studying it.

Anna and Phyllis began to giggle. Nellie and Cotton looked at each other and Phyllis' husband shook his head and said, "Your days are numbered now, pal."

Frankie looked at him puzzled, "What's that mean?"

"Tell him, Phyllis," her husband said, nudging her in the side with his elbow. Anna turned her eyes toward her lap and appeared visibly flustered.

Phyllis told him what the silver ring meant, and Frankie appeared rather nervous as he stroked the ends of his handlebar mustache. "All wives' tales," he said, firmly. He dug his spoon back into the bowl of pudding.

Later they opened the presents and, around ten o'clock, Nellie showed Cotton to the door. Alone and looking at each other, she glanced up to the mistletoe dangling from the top of the doorway. She heard the others in the parlor talking in muffled voices. Cotton looked up and saw the mistletoe. Nervously, they looked at each other, their hearts pounding in tandem.

Cotton's palms were sweating and his mouth had suddenly become dry. Slowly he inched his face toward hers. Their lips met and Nellie felt his rough hands slide around to her back as he pulled her closer to him. Her heart felt like it would jump out of her throat. She felt him letting her go. He stepped back and her warm face looked at him with eyes that saw him in a new and strange way.

"I have to go," he said quickly.

"See me tomorrow?" Nellie whispered.

"Sure." He smiled at her and went out the door.

Nellie watched him walking down the sidewalk, the snow blowing around him in swirls. Closing the door, she leaned her back against it, looking up at the mistletoe and wrapping her arms around herself. She moved her hand up to her throat and gently touched the moonstone necklace Cotton gave her for Christmas. The gem, polished to a brilliant luster set in silver, glistened. Closing her eyes, she tilted her head back, reliving her first kiss.

SEVEN
HEATHER AND HOPE

It was a drizzly April day in 1917, as Cotton and Nellie strolled up the sidewalk in Oak Hill. A large group of people crowded in front of the small wooden building housing the Oak Hill branch of the Wheeling Intelligencer, the only newspaper in town. Their voices buzzed soft with excitement. A newspaper taped to the window of the building faced them.

"Make way," a young boy said, pushing through the crowd, followed by two more running out of the building through an open door. All three of them struggled with arms loaded with newspapers. One of them went north up Main and the other in the opposite direction. The boy who had yelled, obviously the leader of the newsboys, realized that all of his sales were in close proximity of him stayed close to the crowd. With his freckled face turned upward, and his nose crinkled, he yelled in a loud, high-pitched voice, "Read all about it. Read all about it. United States declares WARRRR...!"

"Gimme a paper kid," Cotton said, thrusting out three pennies and grabbing a paper from the kid's hand. Nellie leaned over him and read the bold headlines. She swallowed but the lump in her throat stayed. It was four days before her sixteenth birthday and war had come to Oak Hill.

The ride back to the house in the Model T was silent. The sound of shifting gears and the noise of the engine was all she heard, and even that sounded distant and faraway. War and Cotton plagued her with despair. He dropped her off in front of the house without saying a word and she rushed to the front door.

"Mama, Mama!" she yelled, running through each downstairs room with the newspaper clutched tightly in her hand. Quickly scanning each room with her blue eyes, frightened and wide, she heard the door of the pantry swing open. It was her mother, holding two glass quart jars of green beans in her hands.

"Oh, Mother," she choked on her words, as the pent up tears flooded down her cheeks. "Look, look, we're going to war!" The paper in her hand rattled as she watched her mother's mouth drop open. The jars slipped from Anna's fingers, falling in slow motion. That was the last thing Nellie remembered as she fainted and collapsed in a heap on the dining room floor.

* * *

Nellie counted the minutes before Cotton would be leaving. Each passing day drew her nearer to him. She could not shake the dreadful feeling of what might lay ahead. The time for his departure was coming much too soon for her.

On his last night, they stood in front of the Majestic Theater after the show. Nellie begged him to wait until the draft started in June, but Cotton would have no part of it. Forty-three men had already left Oak Hill and, every time he watched them board the troop train for Virginia and basic training, he wished it was him instead. He'd made up his mind: Tomorrow, it would be his turn.

The July night was warm as they walked slowly back to the boarding house. The star filled sky appeared to light the way, and the newly installed gas lamps lining the walkway whispered hisses at them. The fragrance of wild honeysuckle blew down from the mountains.

"Can you smell that?" he asked.

"Yes, it's such a sweet smell."

She struggled with her thoughts; every step was time, every heartbeat gone forever. They were now out of the sight of shops and houses and into the expanse just before the train station and her house. She had to tell him or risk him never knowing. It will give him hope, she thought, a reason to survive and to come back to her. She stopped in the middle of the sidewalk and cupped his cheeks with both hands. Her blue eyes welling up with tears burned into his, and with a choked whisper, she said it.

"I love you Cotton Pearce."

She held him tight as the tears came. His fingers brushed through her hair and he whispered his promise of love to her. The break of their embrace came slow and they lingered close together. They walked silently, both feeling the bittersweet pain of young love.

Nellie tossed and turned in the sweltering bed that night. The curtains barely moved with what little air came into the room, and even the breeze felt muggy against her skin. She drifted off to sleep with thoughts of Cotton burning in her mind and then she began to dream.

He was standing in a trench looking back at her with a hollow look: His face without any sign of emotion, staring as if he was looking past her. His doughboy helmet was tilted to the side of his head with the strap hanging loosely under his chin. In the dream, she screamed for him to move, but nothing came out. She was filled with terror, pointing frantically for him to look behind. A yellow cloud of mist rolled toward him, enveloping him, and she watched him vanish before her eyes.

Nellie woke sweating more from fear than the heat of the room. She sat up in the bed, wide-eyed. She trembled and looked out the window. The soft light rising over the tops of the mountain showed daylight. She had barely slept at all. She crawled out of bed and went downstairs to the kitchen.

"Good morning, Mama," she said.

"Morning sweetie," Anna said, as she continued to scrub a big iron skillet in the sink. She rinsed the soap off it with a small pail she kept handily by the sink and picked the heavy pan up, holding it by the handle as she dried it with a dishtowel.

"Do you want me to go with you to the station?" Anna asked her.

"I don't think so Mama," she said, "it's something that I feel better facing alone."

"Are you sure?"

"Yes," she said. After all, her mother had always been there for her. This time she felt it was something she just had to handle alone. Nellie bathed and dressed. Cotton had to be at the station at least a half-hour before the eight o' clock troop train arrived.

"How do I look?" Nellie asked her mother as she turned slowly around in a circle. Nellie wore a tiered, powder blue skirt with its hem down to her ankles. Her blouse was white and she had a big, lightweight hat on her head. Her blonde hair, held up with a silver barrette, just touched the back of her neck and framed her triangular face. The moonstone necklace hung from around her neck.

"You look beautiful," Anna said. She straightened the collar on the blouse.

"I'm so afraid, Mama," Nellie said, her voice cracking.

"I know darling, but you have to be strong." Anna stroked her daughter's soft cheek. The tears in her eyes were beginning to well up.

"Don't cry now," she said. "You don't want your nose to turn red, do you?"

Nellie forced a little laugh at the remark and squeezed her mother's hand. She had to be strong. Nellie Blue Bell was not going to cry. She had to tell herself this, repeatedly, as she walked from the house to the station.

Cotton was standing on the platform, his government ticket in his hand. He had on dungarees and a brown shirt. A suitcase rested at his feet. His blonde hair was still damp and his face scrubbed clean. He smiled as she walked closer.

"Hi," Cotton said, showing no outward sign of the nervousness that he felt inside.

"Hello." She reached out and took his hand. There were five or six other couples standing on the platform and a couple of young men with their mothers and fathers.

"How did you sleep?" she asked.

"Good," he said, lying. He had not slept a wink.

"Where's your Mother and Father?" she asked.

"I told them it weren't necessary," he said. He was afraid they would not have enough gas to get back home if they brought him. Besides, his mother was up all night crying and he did not want her to suffer through another long goodbye.

"I'll look out for them if you want," she said.

"That would be mighty nice of ya," he answered.

It was incredibly quiet on the wooden platform leading off the boarding deck of the station. She could sense the anxiety all around her. The people talked in such low voices as if they didn't want anyone else to hear them: Their goodbyes were a private matter. Nellie felt the tension in the air; the sadness and the pain of people saying goodbye.

She knew some were thinking that this would be the last time, the last time they would touch the hands and hear the laughter and voices of these young men full of life. She could hear the chugging of the train, in the distance, coming from the other side of the mountain. It was approaching on the curved portion of the track that circled the base of the mountain.

"Here, take this." Nellie reached into her big shoulder bag and handed Cotton some sandwiches wrapped in wax paper.

The train was rounding the curve, not yet in sight.

"Ya didn't have to," he said.

The chugging of the train grew louder.

"I'm going to miss you so much," she said, clenching her teeth and nearly whispering.

The whistle of the train echoed in her ears, haunting, as it blew its warning at the intersection in Summerlee.

"I'm gonna miss ya too."

The chugging grew louder; drumming in her head as she nervously glanced at the cloud of black smoke beginning to show over the green treetops. The locomotive's cowcatcher began to touch the portion of the track that straightened as it left the hidden curve.

"Write to me."

She held his hand tightly.

The top of the locomotive peeked over the sumac trees.

"I will," he said, his arms moved around her thin waist.

The tracks in front of the station clicked and vibrated slightly. She felt it through the soles of her shoes.

"I'll think of you every day," she said, her lip trembling.

The chugging of the train grew louder in her ears and the smell of the sulfur from the coal boilers began to fill her nose. She watched as the front of the locomotive came into view. Moving steadily, rocking back and forth, she looked at him, then to the train and then back to him. She had never felt so helpless.

The whistle blew loud and long, sending cold shivers up her perspiring back. The chugging slowed in her ears as the engineer throttled the train down, and the hissing of the brakes seemed to shush the murmuring crowd.

She flung her arms around his neck and buried her face against him, sobbing on his chest. "I love you, I love you," she whispered repeatedly. Cotton took her by the wrists and gently moved her back. They looked at each other, embraced, and kissed long.

"All aboard!" the conductor yelled from the bottom of the steel steps of the passenger car. A sergeant in a uniform, his campaign hat pulled down over his eyes, checked each government ticket and marked something on a clipboard in his hand.

Cotton picked up the suitcase and looked at her.

"I gotta go," he said, as if he was merely walking out the front door of her house.

She watched him walk up the steps of the train, his suitcase at his side. He took a seat by the window and looked at her. He mouthed his words through a fingerprint smudged and dusty glass window, "I love you."

The train moved forward and she heard the clunking down the line as the tension pulled on each of the cars' hitches. Slowly the train began to leave the station and Nellie ran along side of it, holding one hand on her wide brimmed hat and waving to him with the other. She stopped at the edge of the platform and watched, with hot tears running down her face, as the caboose disappeared out of her sight. She walked back to the house, carrying her hat in her hand and now feeling very alone.

* * *

The days passed slowly without Cotton. It seemed everything and everywhere reminded her of him. She tried to think of school. She tried to think of anything that would make the pain go away. Finally, with the start of school, she was able to throw herself headlong into her classes. It eased her pained heart for the time being.

The heat in the classroom made it very uncomfortable even with the windows open. It was nearly the end of September and it still seemed like the middle of summer. Nellie's fingers tapped the keys of the Remington manual typewriter, and she listened as the teacher told the girls in the class not to look at the keys, "asdf, asdf, asdf" She looked up at the letters appearing on the heavy paper. "Memorize the home keys," the teacher said. ";lkj ;lkj ;lkj" Nellie's right hand danced across the keys.

"Very nice, Miss Bell," the teacher standing behind her said, "You'll make a fine secretary one day."

It was the last year of high school for Nellie and she was thinking about the school up in Charleston. After all, Aunt Phyllis did tell her mother she could live with them if she so decided. She daydreamed as she typed the home row, practicing each letter repeatedly. Her thoughts turned to Cotton.

She had received two letters from him since he left. The last one was from France. Inside he had put a miniature bouquet of heather, tied together with a piece of string from one of his Army shirts. She wrote to him nearly every day and the typing teacher sometimes let the girls practice by typing letters to some of the boys they knew over there. She looked down at the typewriter paper: "Cotton, Cotton, Cotton" had replaced the home key exercise.

The bell rang signaling the end of the day. The girls in the classroom shuffled their chairs, picked up their books, and were ready to leave when the teacher said, "Wait girls, I have an announcement to make. Please be patient. I know it's hot and you all are anxious to get home." She walked back and forth in front of the class with her hands clasped in front of her.

"In order to do our part for the war effort, we are collecting fruit pits from various restaurants and homes in town. The pits are burned and turned into charcoal. They need the charcoal for the filters in the gas masks. It takes seven pounds of pits for one gas mask. I need volunteers to pass out these mimeographs." She pointed to a stack of papers on the corner of her wooden desk.

"The pits will be picked up by Mr. Grice, the school custodian, and taken over to Charleston once a week. If any of you are interested, I'd appreciate it if on your way out ya'll took some. Thank you."

The young ladies filed out of the room, each of them taking a handful of the leaflets. Nellie took some of the copies and left. Walking through town, she stopped at the company store, the Wonder Bar Diner, and Edmondson's Furniture Store. She walked up the street past the company house that she used to live in. She stopped at it, and then at each row house on the way home, and left a copy. She crossed the dusty street and dropped one off at the rail station, turned, and walked toward home.

She saw the Pearce's automobile parked out in front of the house. Mr. Pearce shouldn't be here, she thought. Her mind began to race. She started to run, and when she reached the porch, she opened the door and ran inside. She threw her hat on the dining room table. Quiet voices were coming from the parlor. She prayed it wasn't about Cotton.

Mr. Pearce and his wife were sitting on the settee. Anna was in one of the matching chairs. Their eyes met hers as she stood in the doorway. Cotton's mother's eyes were red and his father stared at her with a tired look. Her gaze went to the eyes of her mother, also red and moist from crying.

"What?" Nellie said, glancing at the yellow telegram in Mr. Pearce's hand.

"What?" she said again, her voice rising.

"Sit down dear," her mother said in a comforting voice. Nelly walked over to the other empty chair, her heart pounding with fear.

"It's Cotton," Mr. Pearce said.

Nelly leaned forward, listening hard, her heart pounding in her throat and her mouth dry.

"He was in a battle, some place I cain't really say it good. "Moose Argon Forest." He pronounced as it sounded to him. He cleared his throat trying to cover up his embarrassment.

"Anyway, some big woods over there in France."

She knew he meant Meuse-Argonne; they had read about it in current events just last week.

"Well," Mr. Pearce said slowly. "This here telygram sez he's in a hospital, and that he got gassed by them Germans. He's comin home in two weeks."

"How bad is it?" Nellie asked, feeling a bit relieved. She had thought for sure he was dead.

"Don't know. Telygram only says what I done told ya."

Mr. Pearce rose from the chair and helped his wife up. He said, "We're sposed to git something that'll tell us more, maybe in a day er two." They walked to the door and Nellie and her mother followed them out onto the porch. They watched in silence as the Pearce's truck drove off and out of sight.

EIGHT
DAISIES AND DOUBT

The stifling heat of September 1918 faded and the cool nights of October began. The beauty of the mountains, painted in reds, oranges, and yellows, signaled the fall. The Pearces drove to the station to await the arrival of Cotton. Nellie and her mother decided to walk the distance. The last telegram the Pearces received informed them that a nurse would be accompanying Cotton on his journey, all the way from Long Island, New York.

Nellie walked alongside her mother in the bright autumn sun. It was nearly three o'clock and the train would be arriving anytime.

"Come on, Mother," Nellie said, excited and tugging on her sleeve, trying to make her go faster.

"I'm moving as fast as I can go," her mother laughed, sharing in Nellie's joy.

"I'm not getting any younger, you know."

They walked across the street and followed the worn path leading across the grass to the station. The sound of the train's whistle, blowing at the Summerlee crossing, had her hurrying even faster. It would only be a matter of minutes, she thought. She nearly tripped on the wooden steps leading up to the platform in front of the station. She hoped no one saw her, and then, just as quickly, she really didn't care if anyone had.

Just like before, the train was coming around the curve, and she saw the black smoke rising from the stack. At the end of the platform stood the Pearces and she made her way through the small crowd. Her mother hurried behind her.

The train pulled into the station, the locomotive passing the wooden platform, leaving the first passenger car directly in front. The long passenger train had wooden sashes covering the windows. A few windows opened halfway and Nellie craned her neck to see.

A door opened near the front of the car where it connected to the engine, and two burly sergeants in full uniform got off the train. They walked down the steel steps and stood, one on each side of the stairway. Nellie stood on the tips of her toes trying to look over a big man whose shoulders blocked her view. She moved her head from side to side trying to see past him.

A nurse, in a long, white cotton uniform dress, walked off the steps and said something to the two sergeants. Covering her head was a white nurse's hat with a flap in the back attached to a skullcap. A red cross beamed from the front of the white skullcap. She tapped one of the sergeants on the shoulder and walked back up the steps. The two sergeants moved to the top of steps and stood across from each other, their backs tight against the handrails.

The front of a wheelchair poked out the door. The sergeants each held on to the front of the chair and the nurse pushed the wheelchair out on to the flat steel platform at the top of the steps. Nellie heard the murmuring crowd suddenly go silent. She looked at the Pearces who stood staring with open mouths.

Nellie pushed her hands on the back of the man in front of her, nudging him to her left. She had just enough room to squeeze between him and another woman holding a baby wrapped in a blanket. She raised her hand and shaded her eyes from the sunlight reflecting off the bright metal of the passenger car. The sergeants lifted the wheelchair containing the man down the ramp. White bandages hid his eyes, and his arms and legs trembled. He seemed to struggle for air. An olive drab wool robe covered his frail body. Nellie covered her mouth with the palm of her hand. It was Cotton.

They wheeled him to the platform on a makeshift wooden ramp that bridged the last train step with the waiting area. The sergeants walked in front and the people parted, letting them pass through. Behind the nurse a slow parade of men, some limping, some with arms bandaged, and some on crutches, made the effort to meet again with their waiting families.

Nellie watched, stiff with fear, and became more frightened as the wheelchair drew closer. Cotton's head was loosely bobbing as if he were trying to lift it. Anna stood behind her, placing a comforting hand on her shoulder. The wicker wheelchair's wheels squeaked and screeched, its front wheel wobbling wildly along the boards of the platform. She pushed the Pearces out of her way and ran, crying, off the platform toward home.

Anna followed her and found Nellie standing in the front yard. Her face was buried in her hands, and she was sobbing uncontrollably. Anna wrapped her arms around her and tried to console her daughter.

"WHY?" Nellie said. She just could not understand it all.

"Shhh, shhh," Anna said while she gently rocked her in her arms and stroked her hair.

"Let's go inside." Anna tightened her hold around Nellie's shoulders.

Slowly they moved across the yard and up to the porch. Anna helped Nellie upstairs to her room, returning downstairs to make her a cup of sassafras tea.

Nellie was lying on her back on the bed staring up at the ceiling. Tears slowly leaked out the corner of her eyes, and she wondered: What had she done to deserve this? Why did this have to happen to him? She heard her mother coming up the stairs.

"Here, drink this." Anna handed the hot cup of tea to Nellie. Nellie pushed herself up and Anna fluffed up the big feather pillows, sliding them between the headboard and Nellie's back. The cup trembled in her hand and vibrated on the saucer

"Mama, do you think he's blind?" she asked. "I read that sometimes the gas only blinded people for a short time." She took a sip of her tea and set the cup and saucer on her nightstand.

"I'm not sure; I plan to go to the Pearces in a little while. I'm going to take some bread to them and I'll find out. I think the nurse is staying for a week or two," Anna replied, sitting at the foot of the bed, her hands clasped in her lap.

"I can't go, Mama," Nellie said, the tears starting again and her voice shaking. "I don't know what I'd say. He looked so helpless. It just wasn't him."

"You stay in bed, dear. I'll let you know everything when I get back. Frankie is in the back yard working on a waterline to the house.

I'll tell him you're here, and if you need anything, he can take care of you until I get back," Anna said in a tender voice.

"Get some rest."

* * *

It took Nellie nearly a week to summon up the courage to visit Cotton. She turned the faucet on in the new bathroom Frankie installed in the room that used to be the Irishman's rental. He had met one of the local women and tied the knot. The engineer was gone as well, back to Chicago. The Welshman, Frankie, and the Italian were the only three boarders left.

Nellie slid into the white cast iron tub and the cold metal on her back made her gasp, but the hot water soon began to take away some of the anxiety she was feeling. She now knew he was permanently blinded, and the nurse had said that his lungs would never be the same since the gas had scarred the tissues. The attack had come at dawn while Cotton was fast asleep. He had never seen it coming. Everyone said he was lucky to be alive.

The nurse told Nellie's mother he had been asking for her and that it might be good if she came and spent time with him. At least it might help him psychologically. Nellie prepared herself for the meeting, especially since the nurse told her mother that Cotton probably wouldn't be the same person Nellie had known before. She finished her bath and dressed. Frankie now had a used Model T and offered to drive her up to the Pearce's. They lived about a mile away from town, down in the hollow, at the foot of South Mountain.

"Are you ready?" Frankie yelled in his deep voice. He stood at the bottom of the stairs, impatient.

"Almost, I'll be down in a minute," she said.

"Women," he muttered under his breath.

"And just what do you mean by that?" Anna walked up behind him. Frankie smiled at her, embarrassed. He had not heard her come in from the kitchen.

"Aww, nothing really," he said, looking down at this boots, shy and awkward. He liked Anna more than he'd ever let on. What he didn't know was that she felt the same way about him.

* * *

Nellie walked inside the small wooden house alone, feeling apprehensive and very tense. The Pearces stayed on the porch, sitting on the homemade bench and chairs that Mr. Pearce had constructed from bent saplings. He had painted them a rich red and Anna found her chair to be very comfortable. She complimented him on his handiwork. The black and tan coonhound, tied to a tree down by the shed, bawled at the strangers.

"Git in yer house," Mr. Pearce yelled. The dog gave him one last soulful gaze, its ears nearly dragging on the dusty bare circle of dirt it had made from walking around and around out of plain boredom. It lazily disappeared into the shed. Frankie took a drink of the coffee Mrs. Pearce offered and set the cup on the wooden two by four serving as a banister.

"That nurse done spoiled that dog," said Mrs. Pearce. "She was a nice woman an' all, but I was kinda glad to see her go. It sure is nice to have ma' house back agin." She smiled softly, staring out toward the dog's shed. Anna noticed she looked tired.

Inside the house, Nellie slowly made her way into the back room. He sat in the wheelchair, his back toward her and his head pointed in the direction of the creek meandering through the back yard, then flowing down into the thick woods. He didn't hear her coming. She looked around the cluttered room.

A big bed nearly took up all the space, its headboard made from iron and painted a milk chocolate brown. Boxes filled with papers and books were scattered haphazardly around the room. A picture of them, from the apple cider festival, was stuck in the corner of the mirror on the handmade dresser. She noticed the corner of it bent out toward the room.

The room was dark, the only light coming through the bare window. It occurred to her that light would make no difference to him; his world was always dark anyway. She moved closer, slowly, not wanting to startle him. Her shoe nudged a clothbound book laying on the floor and she saw him lift his head.

"Who is it?" he said.

"Me. Nellie."

"What do ya want?" he said. It didn't sound like him to her. His voice was raspy, like a very loud whisper. She moved closer and he started to turn the wheelchair in the direction of her voice. The wheelchair spun facing her.

She saw he was struggling to breathe, his sunken chest rising and falling with each breath. She swallowed hard and stood still. She found herself wondering what to say.

"I came to see how you were doing," she said.

"Whattya care anyway?" he said, his teeth clenched and his eyes covered with a pair of dark glasses. The thin wire frames perched crookedly on his nose. She couldn't see his eyes. She did not want to know what they looked like.

"I just..." she started to say and was interrupted when his fist came crashing down onto the arm of the wheelchair.

"I'm crippled and blind. I cain't breathe, cain't see, I'm finished." He tried to be loud but the rasp in his throat just came out like someone with a bad case of laryngitis.

Nellie stepped back, startled at his outburst. She looked at him. Her hands shook, and she suddenly got the strength to talk back.

"Stop that!" she said, raising her voice and surprising herself. "You have to try. You won't eat, you sit in that wheelchair, and your mother said that you're just giving up." She was angry with him and with herself and felt guilty for talking so bluntly.

"Leave me alone," he said.

He coughed loud, his body stiffening with muscular spasms.

"Get out!"

"Cotton I'm so...so sorr..." she never finished.

"Get the hell out," he said, turning the wheelchair back toward the window.

Nellie turned and walked to the door, turning one last time to look at this destroyed man. She saw the tears slowly rolling down his cheeks. She walked from the room and out to the porch.

"I'm ready now," she said to Frankie. She never let on about the conversation in the room. Nellie thanked the Pearces and they left the hollow. From the backseat, she turned to watch the small house disappear in the dust kicked up by the car. On the way home, Nellie was quiet as her mother and Frankie made small talk in the front seat, intent for her sake, to keep the conversation far away from Cotton.

Later that night, Anna and Nellie were busy in the parlor working on a quilt. Nellie fastened a corner of the quilt in the frame and tightened it until it stretched tight as a drum's head.

"There, is that enough?" she asked.

"Uh huh," Anna said as she sorted through various pieces of cloth for the patchwork design. "This ought to look nice don't you think?" Anna said, holding out a triangular piece of red cloth.

"Sure will," Nellie replied, glancing at the cloth and then back down to the frame where she had already started to sew the two sides to the batting inside.

"Mama, what should I do about Cotton?"

"What do you want to do?" asked Anna, picking up a small blue piece of cloth and turning it over in her hands.

"I just don't know if I feel the same about him, and it's not because of his condition. Soon, I'll be in Charleston at school. I won't be here, and helping Mrs. Pearce with him, well, that's nearly impossible. I feel guilty, and today he made me feel a lot worse. He yelled at me and told me to get out," she said, looking up from her sewing.

"Well, I don't really know what to say, except to follow your heart. I know you care about him and it's doubtful that he will ever be the same. It would be a hard choice to make." Anna looked at Nellie, seeing the confusion on her face, struggling with the decision.

"I don't want to be an old maid, Mama," Nellie said, wrinkling up eyebrows. "But he was so nice to me before. He never swore at me. I just don't know what to do. I'm afraid that he'll think I deserted him if I just go to school."

Nellie pricked her finger with the needle.

"Ouch!" she said wincing and putting the tip of her forefinger in her mouth.

Anna leaned over the quilt and took Nellie's hand. "It's nothing." Nellie picked up a silver thimble, put it on her finger, and went back to sewing.

"I guess it's a decision I'll have to make for myself," Nellie said, exhaling, and wishing things were different. Nellie was used to making decisions on her own now. Her mother had raised her to be independent, and she was, but she hated this. She agonized over the decision, over Cotton, and over the vision of how her life spent with this changed man might end.

"I think I'm going to bed, Mama. It's been a really long day," Nellie said, as she nipped the thread with her straight white teeth, and then tied a small knot where she had left off on her sewing. "I'm not much company. I'm sorry."

"It's all right sweetie, I understand. I just wish I could help you more, but in the end, whatever you decide is going to be your decision and I'll stand beside you either way. I love you," Anna said in a soft voice as Nellie got up from the chair and gently kissed her on the cheek.

"Thank you Mama, I love you too," Nellie said. She turned before she went through the doorway. "Good night."

Frankie came up the cellar steps and almost caught her on the elbow when he swung the door open.

"Oh, I'm sorry," he said, his dark skin actually blushing. "I didn't see you."

"It's fine, you missed me," she said, smiling. "Good night Frankie."

"Good night."

She walked up the steps to her bedroom, thinking how she liked Frankie and how nice he had always treated her mother. She secretly wished that her mother would meet someone. She didn't want her to spend her life alone after all these years. It seemed Anna's only job was to see that Nellie had a good life, and she had done that well.

Nellie picked up one of the daisies from the vase on her nightstand. She looked at the white petals. Plucking them she said, in the quietness of her room, "He loves me, he loves me not," and watched the petals flutter to the floor. The last one left was a "he loves me not."

She opened the nightstand, sliding the door open quietly, and took out her book of pressed flowers. She gingerly removed one of the daisies from the vase and placed it in the book. She no longer doubted her decision about Cotton, but she knew it was something that would scar her forever and leave his memory etched in her soul for eternity.

NINE
FISHING AT BEACON MANOR

Nellie counted the days in Beacon Manor like a convict nearing parole on Devil's Island. Each day grew longer. She welcomed night so she could find some respite from the craziness while asleep. She read every book in the place it seemed, and television bored her. She liked to stimulate her mind and television offered her little in that way.

"Morning Nellie," Elaina said cheerfully. She held a tray with a plate of scrambled eggs and toast on it. A plastic cup of orange juice on the tray shook, nearly sloshing over the side.

"Good morning, Elaina," Nellie said from her chair by the window as she eyed the tray.

"Hungry?" Elaina asked her as she set the tray down and opened up the folding stand.

"Just a little."

"Well, if you eat this, and I mean all of it, then I'll give you a surprise."

"What?"

"I can't tell you right now. It wouldn't be a surprise if I did, now would it?" Elaina said in a teasing sort of way.

"A one-way ticket back to Oak Hill?" Nellie asked, a little smile on her lips, "Now that would be a surprise."

Elaina set the tray on the stand and helped Nellie put a cloth napkin down the front of her green blouse. Nellie smelled the perfume Elaina was wearing. She liked it.

"What's that perfume you're wearing? It smells awfully good," she asked as Elaina stood up. Nellie picked up the fork and jabbed it into the eggs.

"It's called 'Wonderful'," Elaina said as she took a seat on the edge of the bed.

"I used to wear vanilla when I was a young girl. It had the sweetest smell, almost like yours," Nellie said as she lifted the fork to her mouth and began to eat.

"You mean the kind you cook with?"

"Uh huh," Nellie mumbled as she chewed.

"I bet you had all the boys, didn't you?"

"Oh, I had a few admirers in my day," Nellie said, stopping in mid chew. "It was tough to feel for anyone after Cotton. He was special, probably because he was my first kiss."

"Did you ever get married?" Elaina asked, leaning toward Nellie as if they were two young girls at a slumber party.

"Almost."

"Cotton?"

"No, it was a man I met during World War Two. We talked about it and we made some plans, but something happened and, well... I really don't want to hold you up with my goings on," Nellie said.

"I do want to hear about it though," Elaina said, getting up from the bed and smoothing down the front of her white pantsuit. "I have to take Mr. Banks his breakfast this morning. He's not feeling well, so I better get going. I'll be back later and maybe we can talk some more."

She walked out the door and Nellie watched her as she rolled the cart in the direction of Banks' room.

Nellie finished the breakfast and slid the plate to the end of the tray. She looked out the window and watched as the rain came down in a light mist. Lightning flashed in the distant. It will probably rain all day, she thought. She got up from the chair and realized that she was feeling much stronger. Her hip didn't really bother her as much, she thought. She looked at her walker and shook her head, leaving it by the chair, and decided to take a walk through the halls without the use of the walker.

Nellie shuffled through down the hall, her flat-soled shoes making bird-like chirps on the tiles as she made her way to the lobby area. The area was empty and she walked past the television and to the double glass doors. She stood looking out to the parking lot. The pansies lined the sidewalk and their dark purple hue contrasted with the gray cement. She thought how nice they would brighten up her room. She pressed the panic bar across the thick doors. The lock clicked and she pushed on the heavy doors. The nurse at the reception station was busy reading and Nellie double-checked just to make sure she wasn't looking.

The door on the left opened and she walked out into the small area that led to another set of glass doors. As soon as Nellie pressed the panic bar on it, an electronic chime went off on the console in front of the nurse's station.

The young nurse looked at the console. A blinking light alerted her that it was the front door. She looked up, expecting to see a delivery person or someone coming for a family visit. Instead, it was Nellie, just outside the doors, her face to the sky, smiling as the rain pattered on her face. Slowly, Nellie turned in circles, giggling like a child, feeling the cool drops on her face. The nurse rushed from behind her desk and moved quickly through the doors. She took Nellie by the hands and walked her back inside.

"Miss Bell, what on earth are you doing?" the nurse said sternly.

"What did it look like? I was feeling the rain-- just feeling the damn rain. Try it sometime."

The shocked nurse looked at Nellie. Nellie pulled her arm away from the nurse's grip and stormed off mumbling "party pooper." The young nurse looked at her, dumbfounded. Nellie was about to turn the corner when she stopped, looked back at the nurse, and stuck out her tongue. Nellie's echoing laughter filled the hall.

Nellie arrived at her room just in time to see Elaina walking up the hallway, heading in her direction. She crossed the room and lowered herself into her chair. Elaina walked into the room carrying a brown paper bag. It was dark near the bottom where oil had seeped through.

"Here's your surprise, sweetie."

Elaina held the bag out in front of Nellie.

Nellie took the paper bag from Elaina's hand and set it on her lap. She opened it a bit, peeking inside. A wide smile broadened on her face.

"Peanut butter cookies. Thank you so much," Nellie said, sniffing the aroma of the cookies rising up from the bag.

"I made them from scratch, because I knew you liked them," Elaina said.

"Warm, too. I know you didn't bake them here," Nellie said.

"Micro-waved them in the break room for you," Elaina said.

"You're a doll, kid," Nellie said, reaching out and patting her on the upper arm.

"I hope you enjoy them," Elaina said, turning and walking toward the door.

"Oh, you don't have to worry about that," Nellie said, as she watched Elaina cross the open door.

"See ya tomorrow," Elaina said from the hall.

"Bye," Nellie replied.

The cookies were soft and the crystals of the white sugar clung to the criss-cross designs on the tops, where Elaina had used the tines of a fork. Elaina made her feel special, treated her like a mother, unlike her own daughter. She had not heard from her since two days after Mother's Day. She had left a message at the front desk, saying she couldn't make it for the visit because her new hubby had an important meeting. "Lard ass lawyer," she said to herself sarcastically. Nellie chuckled. She liked the way it sounded and repeated it out loud again, "Lard ass lawyer."

Nellie had come to terms about her daughter over the last few months. She wondered many times why her daughter had turned out to be the gold-digging, arrogant person that she was. Bad genes from the evil man who fathered her, she figured. Barbara cared about one person and that was herself, Nellie thought. Nellie had given her the best that she could provide and, in return, received nothing but grief from the woman.

Once, Nellie asked her if she was ever going to give her a grandchild. The answer still rang in her ears every time she thought about it: "Why should I? It would just take away from my fun, and I'm not about to share any of my men with a snot-nosed brat."

Nellie's knuckles turned white as she gripped the chair, remembering her daughter's high pitched whining voice. She was determined not to let Barbara bring her spirits down. She was feeling revitalized and attributed it to her journal. She refused to think about Barbara.

I think I'll eat in the dining room tonight, she thought. I'm not going to let anyone bother me and I'm going to enjoy myself. She looked at the clock on the stand by the bed. It was nearly suppertime. She rose from the chair and, without her walker, made her way to the dining area.

"Mademoiselle, mind if I join you?" Banks said, leaning over her. Nellie sat in a chair, watching as he moved around the table.

"Help yourself, Private," she said.

What the hell, she thought, if I can't beat them at their stupid game, I might as well join them and make it a little fun. Banks slid a chair out and sat down directly across from her.

The servers moved around the tables scattered in the dining area and set the plates in front of the residents. A plate of fish was set in front of Nellie. She looked at the flaky meat, sprinkled with just a dusting of paprika. It actually looked good and smelled delicious. She turned the tines of the fork and scraped the fish, watching it fall apart. Lifting it to her mouth, she chewed it slowly, savoring the flavor. She watched as Banks looked at her. She gave him a grin and licked some of the butter off the top of her lip, sultry like.

One of the aides placed a dinner plate in front of Mr. Banks. Nellie looked at it. He was having fish, too. Her appetite was back and she ate the fish on her plate hurriedly. She studied the fish on Banks' plate and alternately glanced between him and the piece of broiled fish, watching as he slowly unfolded his napkin and placed it across his lap. She looked back down at the fish. She found it more appealing than Banks. Finishing the last bite of hers, she noticed Banks continued to fiddle with the napkin on his lap.

"General Pershing! Why, what a surprise," Nellie said, moving her head trying to see around Banks' shoulders. Banks' eyes widened and his shoulders stiffened.

Private Gordon Banks, showing off his best military bearing, turned in his chair, letting his napkin float to the floor and feebly, but quickly, got to his feet. He turned in the direction that Nellie had been looking and brought his right hand up in a salute. Nellie could see his back. He was standing rigid and tall, striking a perfect pose. Without clinking a piece of glassware, she reached over and switched her plate containing tator-tots for his.

Banks continued looking. He missed seeing the General. He turned back around and slid back in his chair. He didn't bother picking up the napkin that lay underneath his shoe. He dug his fork into the tator-tots. He was trying to remember what his fish had tasted like.

Nellie finished her meal and got up from the table. "Au revoir," she said to Banks, as she stepped back from the table. He looked at her blankly, a chunk of a tator-tot dangling off his bottom lip. It slid off, landing in his lap.

"Tsk, tsk. You should try using a napkin. It's not so messy," Nellie said, winking at him. She turned and walked back to her room.

The familiar sound of the cart echoed in the hallway and Nellie listened to muffled arguments over medicine as the nurse made her rounds. The Angel of Mercy dispensed this and that for the residents. Pain killers and brain killers. She finally made it to Nellie's room. Nellie had her method down to a science. It was always the same. Stuff the pills in the chair, get the book, and store them in the hiding place within the cloth cover. She could have won an award for "Best Dramatization of Someone Hating the Taste of Medicine in the category of Wincing and Hard Swallowing". Tonight made fourteen of the blue pills stuffed in the book.

Another nurse at the front desk was sorting through the mail that the residents received. She separated each letter by room number and piled them neatly in little stacks. When she turned as she answered the ringing telephone, she never saw the certified letter addressed to Ms. Nellie Blue Bell slip off the smooth counter. Nor did she notice it as it fluttered like a dropped feather, back and forth through the air, until it landed on the slick, waxed floor with enough momentum to slide under the big copier and come to rest against the baseboard, hidden totally from view.

Nellie sat back in her chair, recalling the fish escapade in the dining room. She smiled a little, remembering the look on Banks' face. She felt good, alive and well, in old folk's hell. She picked up her book, opening it to a new page. A dusty gold tassel, with a charm and a piece of baby's breath wrapped in waxed paper, caught her eye. The small white blossoms, long since discolored, looked like wild mustard. She looked at the beautiful handwriting at the bottom of the page. "Frankie and Anna, December 8, 1919". She reclined back in the chair, and returned once again back to West Virginia, leaving behind Beacon Manor for just awhile.

TEN
BABY'S BREATH AND BETROTHAL

Nellie packed the last of her things in the cumbersome, brown camel-backed trunk. She closed the heavy lid and slid the key into the brass lock. Looking around the sweltering room, she made one last check. She had everything. She slid the wooden framed window down, it screeched until it rested tightly on the sill.

She focused her eyes on the mountain off in the distance, sadly coming to the realization it would be some time before she saw this view again. The familiar sight had greeted her in the mornings and seemed to wish her a goodnight. She loved it in the early morning when the sun would sneak up over the treetops at the back of the mountain and its rays would spike out in all directions. She slowly drew the shades.

She looked at the pendant watch dangling down the front of her blouse. It was almost one o'clock and the train was due at three. She hurried down the stairs to the kitchen.

"I'm just about finished, Mama. Let's sit out on the porch for awhile," she said, watching her mother drying her hands on a dishtowel.

"I think that's a good idea. It's awfully hot in here," Anna said. She hung the dishtowel through the handle of the sink drawer and went outside. The heat of August smacked them in the face like a blast furnace.

"Oh how I wish it would rain," Anna said, wiping the sweat off her brow and settling down in the big wooden rocker.

"It's been about three weeks since we had a drop of rain. Just look at those tomatoes," Nellie said pointing toward the little garden that Frankie had put in at the corner of the yard. The stunted plants drooped with wilted leaves that had turned brown on the tips. Nellie sat in the straight-backed, cane-bottomed chair and straightened her legs out, crossing them at the ankles.

"Are you excited about Charleston?" Anna asked. The rocking chair tapped time on the floor of the porch.

"Sort of, but I'm a little scared too."

"It's a lot bigger than Oak Hill, that's for sure, but your aunt and uncle are good people. I can only hope they don't spoil you," Anna said chuckling. She knew if anyone had spoiled Nellie, she was to blame. However, the years of being a protective mother hen did not exclude certain rules and values.

"That's not what I'm worried about. It is being away at school that bothers me most," Nellie said sadly.

"You'll do just fine. I have faith in you. You didn't become the valedictorian of your high school by luck, now did you?"

"I guess not, Mama. I'll get used to it. It will just take me some time, that's all," Nellie said. She casually flicked her thin fingers at a fat bumblebee trying to land near her. It fanned an angry buzz at the forced flight plan change, landing instead on the white column. Its legs danced on the brilliant white, as if it landed on a frying pan, and it zipped away.

"How would you feel about some lemonade?" Anna asked.

"Sure, why not? I have time."

Anna went into the house and Nellie looked toward the rail station. The sun beat down on the peaked roof of it, and shingles shimmered with waves of heat. A clanking coal train with a hundred cars lumbered slowly on its way down the narrow gauge tracks beside the empty rails reserved for the passenger trains. The wheels rolled over the joints of the rails and ticked like a slow clock in Nellie's head.

The peaks of coal on each car caught the hot sun and glittered like diamonds. The last swaying car passed the station and the building blocked her view. The tons of coal came from the very piece of earth where she was born. Anna returned with the lemonade.

Frankie pulled up to the house in his black Model T. He jumped out of the car and briskly walked toward the gate. He had finished his shift down at the mine. He still wore his leather miner's hat, bent and twisted from water. A brass colored lamp with a reflector on top looked like a third eye as he walked up the steps. Frankie's face was black with coal dust and he reached up on his helmet and slid the lamp off where it fastened with a clip.

"Well, city girl, are you about ready?" he said smiling. His teeth looked bright against his black beard and the coal dust on his face.

"I need some help with the trunk, if you don't mind," Nellie said. She watched as Frankie unscrewed the lid of the brass lamp. He tapped the bottom half of it against the side of the step, dumping out the mixture of water and used carbide near the foundation of the porch.

"Frankie, I wished you wouldn't do that," Anna said, "I told you it kills the grass."

"Sorry," he said shrugging his shoulders like an oversized kid, "I forgot."

Frankie spread the carbide around with the toe of his boot. He looked up with an air of innocence and searched her face for approval. She looked at him, smiling and shaking her head.

"I'll bathe and get your trunk, and then we'll drive it over to the station," Frankie said, screwing the two pieces of the carbide light back together.

"Well, I'm leaving on the three o'clock passenger, so you'll have to hurry," Nellie said.

"I'm gone already now," Frankie said, his English broken. Anna helped him with his English, but on occasion, he seemed to revert to his way. She taught him how to write and to read. He was still learning. Anna was proud of him, and her feelings were growing stronger for him every day.

With the trunk loaded, they drove to the station. Nellie picked up her ticket at the window inside the building. She walked across the floor of the station and sat on the long wooden bench. Frankie and her mother stood by the window, looking out toward the tracks. There was one older woman sitting across from Nellie, a battered suitcase at her feet. Nellie looked at the ticket and then glanced toward the bottom of the bench the older woman was sitting on. A half of a peanut shell was on the floor, pieces of dust stuck to it.

Nellie thought of the night, on this very bench, that Cotton had bought the roasted peanuts and shared them with her. She swallowed hard, sadness deep in the pit of her stomach. The vision was in her head moving like she was at the picture show. She hadn't seen much of him since he told her to get out. Someone had said that he was not doing well. There was talk about putting him in the home for veterans over in Martinsburg.

Maybe it would be better for him, she thought. She knew he probably wouldn't stand for it though. Nellie wondered why things had to turn out the way they did, or why Cotton ended up like he did, or why they had a war for that matter.

He'd never run the hills again, or see the leaves change. She couldn't shake the guilt she felt, no matter how hard she tried. I shouldn't blame myself, she thought. Even Mama said there was nothing I could do. The whistle of the train as it neared the Summerlee crossing shook her back to reality.

Nellie said her goodbyes quickly. She didn't want to make it any harder than it already was. Her mother had started to sniffle just when the train came into sight. Frankie had to put his arms around her to comfort her. He was still holding her close as Nellie looked out the window and watched them grow smaller as the train picked up speed, distancing her from them and Oak Hill. She settled back in her seat and, in a short time, the rocking of the train lulled her into a deep sleep.

* * *

"Next stop, Kanawha City and Charleston."

Nellie woke with the sound of the conductor's booming voice as he walked up the aisles of the car. She rubbed her eyes and looked out into the blackness, bedecked with glittering lights. She felt the train slowing and heard the hiss of steam from the brakes. The station was huge, at least ten times bigger than the one back in Oak Hill, and built of fine red brick.

Nellie scanned the cement platform that ran the entire length of the building and was awed at the hundred or more people milling about. Porters scurried around in blue-gray uniforms, pulling and pushing wooden bottomed carts, some filled with luggage and some empty.

She slid out of the bench seat, picking up her shoulder bag and walking down the aisle toward the exit. The older woman from the

Oak Hill station was in front of her and moving slowly. She wished she would hurry. Nellie looked out the line of windows as she walked up the aisle, hoping to spot her uncle in the sea of faces. Finally, they had reached the metal steps that led off the train. The old woman disappeared into the crowd and Nellie stepped down onto the platform, looking anxiously for a familiar face.

"Over here!"

She looked in the direction of the voice and could see a man jumping to gain some height, waving his hand in the air. It was her Uncle Jim. She breathed a sigh of relief, making her way in his direction as she felt people bumping into her.

"Uncle Jim, I made it," she said.

"Well, I'm glad and so is Aunt Phyllis. She's so excited, even fixed you a room upstairs and went out and made me buy a new bed for you."

Together, they worked their way through the crowd and over to a section of the platform where a black man in a porter's uniform was unloading one of the carts. He was lifting the various suitcases and trunks off of it and lining them up against the wall. Nellie saw her trunk, the last one on the cart. The porter reached out to grasp the leather handle and slide the bulky trunk off.

"Wait," Nellie's uncle said, "We need this one out front."

"Yes sir, I'll follow you with it," the porter said. He straightened his crooked hat and grabbed the trunk by the handle.

They walked through the bustling station. Nellie found herself mesmerized by the size of it; with its polished marble floor and bright lights. She looked up at the high ceiling, noting the beautiful tinwork. A huge chandelier hung from the center of the ceiling. She stayed close to her uncle as they made their way through the massive station.

Once outside, she watched the porter and her uncle struggling with the heavy trunk, finally getting it into the back seat of the sleek, long, black automobile. The porter held out his hand and her uncle slipped him a few coins. Things sure were different here, she thought. On the drive to her new home, Nellie stared with wonderment at the lights, sights, and sounds of Charleston.

"Well this is it," he said, turning the wheel of the automobile into a circular drive and parking in front of the house.

"It's beautiful," Nellie said. The huge brick house had a porch wrapping the entire way around it. Two gaslights lit up the sidewalk with perfectly manicured boxwoods aligned in rows on either side. Aunt Phyllis stood on the porch looking in their direction.

Suddenly, a man appeared in the doorway of a small, two-room guesthouse on the right side of the expansive lawn. He walked underneath a huge silver maple tree in the front of the lawn and ended up on the sidewalk heading toward them. It was her uncle's hired handyman.

"Bags, sir?" he said to Nellie's uncle. His eyes quickly looked her way and back to Uncle Jim.

"Yes, but I'll have to help you with the trunk. It's very heavy."

The two men slid the trunk out from the back seat. She followed behind them as they carried it down the sidewalk and up onto the porch.

"Nellie, I'm so glad you made it, you'll have to catch me up on all the news," Phyllis said excitedly as she embraced Nellie.

"Thank you Aunt Phyllis," Nellie said, as her aunt stepped back crossing her arms and looking her up and down.

"I can't believe how much you've grown. You definitely have you father's height, and that hair, well that's from our side of the family. You look very pretty, a lot like your mother. Don't you think so, Jim?" He didn't answer. He and the handyman had already moved the heavy trunk into the house and were halfway up the wooden staircase with it.

"That man has more energy than anyone I ever saw," Phyllis said, laughing.

"Well, don't just stand there, staring girl. Come on in." She tugged on Nellie's sleeve, leading her to the door like an excited schoolgirl. Nellie thought how she reminded her of her mother and knew that it was going to be all right.

* * *

Three weeks after Nellie arrived; she started classes at the business school. It was on that first Friday, and she had just walked through the door, that her aunt came running out of the parlor, smiling and waving an envelope in her hand. Nellie looked at her and watched her aunt dancing a jig in the foyer.

"You'll never believe it, you'll never believe it, Nellie," Phyllis said, in a high-pitched squeal.

"What Auntie? What?" Nellie repeated, smiling as she watched her contagious excitement.

"Sit, sit," her aunt said, pointing to the walnut chair just inside the foyer. Nellie set her books on the hall tree and quickly walked over, sitting down on one of the walnut chairs that matched the dining table. Her aunt's hand trembled as she handed Nellie the envelope postmarked Oak Hill.

Nellie lifted the flap of the small envelope and slid out a gilded post card. The front of the card embossed with two cherubs floating in space, their chubby hands connecting them together with a round gold band. Nellie turned the card over and read.

Frank Zabbata and Anna Bell request the honor of your presence
At their wedding at Bell's Boarding House
In Oak Hill, West Virginia at 2:00 p.m on Sunday, December 8, 1919.

Nellie squealed loudly and jumped up from the chair, hugging her aunt. She squeezed her tightly and jumped back waving the envelope and saying with a very happy voice: "I knew it, I knew it all along. I have to buy a dress and I have to ..."

"We'll take care of all that, don't you worry," Aunt Phyllis interrupted.

"Frankie is a nice man for her," Nellie said, "They get along so well."

"I'm very happy for her; she deserves it after all she's been through. Maybe now she can get away from all the work of running that boarding house. Let's call her right this minute," Phyllis said, running to the wall phone. Nellie was right behind her, still clutching the invitation and watching as her aunt quickly turned the crank on the side of the wooden phone attached to the wall. She got an operator who connected her quickly, and the three women talked for an hour about the upcoming wedding.

They decided to drive to Oak Hill for the wedding since it had been a mild winter and, besides, Uncle Jim needed to stop to pick up some more liquor for the bar and liquor store he owned on Duffy Street, two blocks from the capitol building.

"I swear that those politicians can drink more bourbon than the men can from the glass plants," he said, his eyes glued to the road and trying to miss as many potholes as he could.

"Don't surprise me at all," Phyllis said, "Some of the laws those politicians come up with...well...a man could only be half drunk to think like that."

Nellie laughed from the back seat at the remark. She'd never set foot inside the bar. It just wasn't a proper thing for a young lady to do in Charleston. Nellie looked out the window and watched the farms passing by.

She thought of her mother's wedding tomorrow and, even though she was happy and liked Frankie, it saddened her when she thought of the man who had given her the middle name that matched the color of her eyes. Nellie had a memory and she would never let it go. The vision of her father was as clear as if it had been yesterday, even though it had been thirteen years since he had passed.

She wondered what he would look like now. She remembered him being handsome. She wondered what he would have thought about her going to school, away from Oak Hill and into a city. Her stomach felt funny. She always had that little tickling sensation, a mixture of joy and sadness blended together, when she thought of him. The joy for having him for the short time that she did, and the sadness for the awful finality of what his death meant. She fell asleep in the back seat of the automobile and didn't wake up until they reached Oak Hill.

* * *

The wedding took place in the parlor of the boarding house. The preacher stood in front of the fireplace with an open Bible in his hands. Frankie fidgeted with a button on his black wool suit. The rest of the small group stood when Anna and Nellie walked into the parlor. Anna wore a dark blue dress with puffy sleeves. She wore a wrist corsage of two roses with a small spray of baby's breath. She had cut her hair for the occasion and it just covered her ears.

Nellie walked her mother to the end of the rug. Every eye in the room was on them as they neared the spot where Nellie would let her go alone. She saw the little chalk mark on the floor, put there earlier to let her know that beyond the mark was the area where the bride and groom would stand. One more long slow step and she stopped. She swallowed hard and looked down into her mother's face. A trembling smile appeared on Anna's face.

This is it, the moment where I give her away. She looked into her mother's blue eyes shining with tears. She held Anna's hands in hers and felt the heat and sweat that seemed to radiate into her own.

She bent down slightly and kissed her mother's soft cheek, smelling the fragrance of lavender soap.

"I love you, Mother," she whispered softly in her ear.

She very slowly felt the touch of her mother's hand slipping from hers, felt the smoothness on her palms as her mother's hand glided through them. Their fingers parted leaving only a ghostly space that she knew could only mean... forever.

ELEVEN
BLEEDING HEARTS AND BROKEN HEARTS

Nellie concentrated on the paper for school. She picked up the pen, poised the nib above it, and began to write. Her beautiful handwriting flowed across the page. Outside, sleet fell and pinged on the roof of the house.

Nellie paused again, this time wondering what time Jim and Phyllis would be home. They left early in the morning and had spent all day putting the final touches on their newly remodeled restaurant and delicatessen. Prohibition had forced them to change it from a bar to the restaurant. Nellie knew Uncle Jim still sold West Virginian hooch out the back door to his political friends, but she never let on.

A thud from outside startled her, and she rose from the chair. Uncle Jim and Aunt Phyllis rarely used the back entrance. She slid the curtain back and scanned the dark back yard. To the right, in the dim light shining from the window of the guesthouse, a shadowy figured moved about inside. The handyman gave her the jitters. Nate Martin gave many people that feeling.

The thirty-year-old handyman moved from Huntington to Charleston to find employment. He told Nellie that much. He did not tell her lying low from the law was another reason.

Nate was short and thin. His black hair appeared greasy most times, and his face showed pockmarks. His twisted nose pushed to the right side of his face, and was probably caused, she thought, by drunken brawling. After all, the few times he spoke to her, she smelled the liquor on his breath. However, the feature that she noticed most of all was his eyes. Gray and small, they stuck out of his head like the eyes of mouse squished in a spring trap.

Inside the guesthouse, Nate busily filed off the sharp burrs of metal on a freshly cut piece of pipe. He broke the wooden handle of the snow shovel in the early morning and decided to replace it with an old piece of pipe left over from the installation of natural gas in the main house. He filed hard, making boar-like grunts with each stroke.

Nate set the file down and walked to the front of the guesthouse. He lifted his mattress and pulled out a Mason jar half full of moonshine. Walking over to the window that faced the main house, he slid the curtain back again. This time he could see she was standing. A bonus, he thought, as the light outlined her smooth curves. He checked the position of the shovel handle he kicked over earlier. The thud on the wall of the guesthouse sent him scurrying, but this time he did not want the show interrupted. His perverted entertainment ended when she turned away and the light in the room went off.

Tires crunching on the driveway sent Nellie down the stairs. She heard their voices and relief washed over her. At the foyer she watched them walking up the drive, laughing. An unlikely couple, but the happiest Nellie ever knew.

Uncle Jim was nearly bald, with a round red face and perpetual smile. Her aunt looked almost like her mother, all the Swedish features, but taller and she always marcelled her short, blond hair. It glistened in the porch light.

"Why hello, sweetheart," Uncle Jim said. He talked loud through the clear leaded glass of the front door, "Did a little celebrating, we did!"

He staggered back a step and Phyllis steadied him with a hand on his elbow. Nellie opened the door and his shoulder bounced off the doorframe as Phyllis guided him in.

Inside, Phyllis took off his heavy coat and hung it on the hall tree. He wobbled watching her with his amusingly crooked fedora sliding on his head. He was humming an old Irish song. Nellie followed them into the living room.

"Well, the restaurant officially opens tomorrow," he said, sitting upright in the chair, and then slowly leaning to the right.

"That is great, Unc," Nellie said. She was excited for the both of them. She slid out a chair and sat. Her eyes followed her Aunt who walked to the kitchen to fetch some coffee.

"Wanna job, part time?" Uncle Jim said. Nellie turned to face him, her eyebrows raised.

"I'd love to have a job," she said. "Doing what?" She asked.

"Office work. You're good with figures and Phyllis and I could use your help," he said.

"Phyllis, come out here please," he slurred.

Phyllis walked from the kitchen balancing a cup and saucer in her hand. Setting it in front of Jim, she sat down in a chair next to him. Her elbow was on the table and she leaned her face tiredly in her hand.

"What is it dear?" she said.

"Remember our conversation about hiring Nellie?"

"Of course, it was only a ten minutes ago, in the car." She winked at Nellie.

"Well, tell her all about it. I'm going to bed. I drank too much corn liquor and I... uh," he yawned wide. Pushing his hands on the tabletop, he pushed up on wobbly legs. He staggered to the stairs. The two women watched his fedora fall and roll off his back. He grasped the handrail, pulling himself up each step.

"Night all," he yelled from the top of the stairs. The door to his room closed.

They looked at each other and laughed loudly as Phyllis got up and put the fedora on her head and imitated his stagger all the way to the hall tree and hung up the hat. Phyllis told her about the job, the pay, and how many hours it might require. Nellie listened intently and asked her if she could call her mother tomorrow and tell her the good news. She might have to finish school part time, but it would put money in her pocket and she liked that idea.

* * *

It was in March when the letter arrived with the return address of the Pearces scrawled in lead pencil. Cotton asked them to write to her. The poorly written letter, with misspelled words, apologized for what he had said and that he wanted to set things right. She had written to him several times since coming to Charleston, but she had forced herself, through sheer determination, not to dwell on the pain.

She wrote short, curt letters telling him about school and hoping that he would come to grips with his destiny. Never once did she tell him she loved him. She felt that it would lead him into believing that there was a chance for them. There wasn't. She knew she could not live the kind of life she would have with him. She wanted to achieve something and, even though she sometimes felt riddled with guilt, she had to let go.

Later that day, Nellie sat at the dining room table. The ringing phone sent her rushing to answer it. She expected the call from her Uncle and had waited for over an hour.

"Hello," she said.

"Mother, I'm so glad to hear from you," she said, "What a nice surprise."

She listened, and then gripped the top of the phone. Her former beaming face, thinking it was Uncle Jim, changed to puzzlement. She turned, slumping against the wall.

"No!" she screamed into the receiver.

"I just got a letter from him today," she said. Tears streamed down her face and she choked out, "he couldn't have."

Her mother's voice provided the only comfort in the empty house. Her sobs filled the room. They slowed, with her mother explaining to her that at least his suffering had ended. The sights of him struggling with each breath, and his frustrated wishes to be whole again, came back to her. Her mother was right. Red-eyed, she listened and somehow understood.

They talked about Cotton as a younger boy. They reminisced about the good things and spoke of the Christmas tree they brought home in that cold winter. They each shared memories and spoke little of what the war made of him. Finally, Nellie hung up the phone and went upstairs, crying herself to sleep.

She could not attend the funeral. Her classes and work had taken priority, especially since she was having finals. She tried, but it was something they told her she could not make up unless it had been a death in the immediate family. She did not bother to ask the dean; she knew what the regulations were. She wrote to the Pearces, expressing her sorrow and explaining why she could not be there. All she could do was hope that they would understand.

At the end of April, she returned to Oak Hill. Nellie stood in front of the grave looking at the hand chiseled headstone made from a flat boulder of river rock. The rock was dyed orange from the sulphur seeping from the mines to the river and gave it a distinctive color. She looked at the mound of black dirt and bent down, brushing away the wilted flowers piled near the headstone.

The sun burned the drops of dew off the grass surrounding her. She had picked the bleeding hearts out of the back yard of her mother's home and placed the bouquet on the top of the mound. She stood back feeling the fingers of breeze on the back of her neck.

The cemetery was empty except for Nellie and the wind. She thought about Cotton and his short life. She tried to imagine his thoughts when he picked the squirrel gun up in his hands, how he probably fumbled around in his blackness until the muzzle was in his mouth. She thought she had known him. She did know him back then, but not the man he had become.

"Goodbye Cotton," she whispered and turned, walking away from the grave and leaving behind a part of her life that she chose to lock away in her heart.

* * *

Nellie worked obsessively at the restaurant; it was her therapy. She attended school three nights a week and still maintained the highest standing in her class. Her uncle set up an office for her in the back room of the restaurant. There was a wooden desk, chairs, and pictures on the wall. It was her office and she ran it in such a manner that Uncle Jim almost felt like he worked for her. He didn't care. She had cut costs and scheduled things so efficiently that the place profited twice as fast as he had projected.

Nellie realized she was taking so many accounting courses outside the secretarial realm of the school that she could earn a degree in business and marketing instead. The girls in her classes often times told her she was wasting her time, because only men worked in those jobs. She ignored their words, remarking on more than one occasion, "just watch me." The girls did watch her, more than once, as she walked confidently into a room filled with male students. Once, when she was the only one to ace a very difficult marketing exam, even the male students applauded her.

One of the male classmates invited her out for dinner. She declined. After Cotton, she decided her career would take precedence and she would wait for Mr. Right. If he came along: fine. If not, she thought, there would be plenty of time for that. She liked men and their attention, but unlike most of the women she knew, it was not her priority.

A few weeks before the end of the semester, Nellie found herself working late into the night. She was balancing the day's receipts from the restaurant. It was quiet, her Aunt and Uncle had left hours ago. She banded the last stack of bills with a rubber band and snapped it loud against the bills. "Done," she sighed.

Putting the money in the safe, she gave the combination a spin and tested the security with a quick pull on the handle. She locked the front door and walked to the waiting jitney she had called earlier. Silvery plumes of exhaust puttered from the tailpipe into the cool night air. She climbed into the back seat and the driver took her home.

Back at the house she didn't notice the curtain in the guesthouse sliding back, and she didn't feel the mouse eyes of Nate Martin as he watched her walking up the sidewalk and into the house. He slid the curtain back and took a long swig from the glass jar. He licked his lips and parted his yellowed teeth, sucking air through the gaps to cool off the heat of the shine. He whispered to himself in a heavy tongued drawl, "Gonna git it, gonna git it."

Cackling a little too loud for his criminal comfort, his greasy hand covered his mouth, as paranoia set into his moonshine dulled brain. He staggered to his bed, lifted the mattress and dropped the jar on the open springs with a ringing metallic "boing". Reaching up, his fingers pulled the chain on the light.

He stepped to the bed and collapsed on it, sweating profusely and fantasizing in the darkness about the three young women he had raped back in Huntington. Two of his victims took his threats seriously, and fear kept them from reporting it to anyone. The third one, that whiny mouthy bitch as he recalled, would never tell a soul. He made sure of that. Sliding the pillow from behind his head, he clutched it tight to his chest. The gaslights from the sidewalk painted the soft square of the window on his pockmarked face. Turning toward the window, a slow smile grew with the pressure of his finger-tightening grip on the dirty pillow

TWELVE
LILIES, LIES, AND LABOR

Nellie took the summer off from school to work at the restaurant. She saved her money, set on buying a used Model T automobile. Few women drove automobiles, but she also did not care what other women did. She knew what she wanted.

With the war over, out went the pork-less Saturdays. Since it was her day off, Nellie decided to surprise her uncle and aunt with a pork roast. She seasoned the big piece of meat, lowering it into the heavy iron pot. Her blue eyes watered as she cut the big onion and placed the rings on the sides and top of the meat.

With both hands, she lifted the heavy pot and carried it from the sink to the stove. She struck a wooden match on the sole of her shoe, twisted the porcelain handle, and dropped the burning match down a hole near the front of the hissing open oven. The familiar, "Whoomph," resounded in the kitchen with the ignition of the gas. She slid the pot in and closed the oven door.

Outside, Nate Martin cut the grass with a push mower and the noise of the whirring blades drifted up to the open window. The hot June weather required him to mow the thick green carpet at least once a week. Nellie wiped her hands on a hand towel by the sink and looked out. She watched him stop and bend down, inspecting the machine. He dropped to his knees and scraped the sticking grass off the blades with a flat stick. He stood up and continued pushing in a straight line, turning at the back of the yard by the fence and then mowing toward the house. He looked up and saw her. He waved to her and she acknowledged him with a nod of her head.

The sun was shining brightly and the heat from the oven was making the kitchen a little too warm for her comfort. She reached out and pushed the window up as far as it would go. He looked up at her and she caught his gaze. He quickly looked down at the spinning blades of the mower as if he was embarrassed. She noticed he was red faced and sweating. The short-sleeved shirt he wore was unbuttoned revealing his pale white skin. Nellie walked to the icebox, taking out the glass pitcher of fresh lemonade she had made earlier.

She picked up the wooden handled ice pick from the top of the oak cabinet and chipped away at the block of ice in the bottom of the icebox. At the sink, she dropped the cold chunks into a tall glass. She filled it with the lemonade and dried the outside of the glass with the hand towel.

Leaning over the sink, she yelled down to him.

"Would you like a glass of lemonade?"

He quickly looked up, startled for a moment, and his mouth opened in a slow grin. He nodded his head in acceptance. Drops of sweat flew from his greasy hair from the motion. He leaned the handle of the mower against the side of a tall magnolia tree and took out a filthy handkerchief, wiping his hands and the sweat from his pockmarked face.

She heard his heavy boots on the porch. He opened the front door and stepped inside. She did not hear the click of the lock since he covered the sound with a loud, faked cough. He walked into the kitchen.

Nellie handed him the glass of lemonade and he sat down at the small drop leaf oak table. He took a long gulp of the ice cold drink and set the glass on the table.

"Thank you, ma'am," he said, breathing hard as he slid his dirty finger up the side of the glass leaving a clear, finger-wide streak.

"You're welcome," she replied.

Nellie turned back to the sink, picking through a porcelain white basin of potatoes. She separated the good ones from those having sprouts beginning to grow on them. The good potatoes landed with a thump in the sink.

He looked at her shoulders, exposed where her cotton dress hung loose forming a slight v-shape that showed the ridges of her vertebra. Her blonde hair was off her neck and covered with a white kerchief, tied in the front and the point aiming toward the base of her neck. He turned his gaze to the ice pick with the well-worn handle sticking over the wooden top of the icebox. Calmly, he took another drink from his glass.

"Mighty warm out there today," he said. His mouse eyes traveled down her back slowly.

"It sure is," she said, speaking without turning and washing one of the potatoes under the running faucet.

The curtains fluttered as a breeze pushed through the open window. Nellie shut the water off, taking the last potato and placing it with the rest of them on a towel spread out on the left side of the sink. She picked up the hand towel and dried her hands.

He slowly shifted his work-boots on the floor, testing to see if they would make any sound. She looked out the window and watched a goldfinch zipping with an up and down path through the air then landing on a branch of the magnolia.

Nate rose, slowly straightening up. He kept his gray eyes focused on her. He reached over the drop leaf table and cleanly picked the ice pick up silently from the wooden top of the icebox. Quietly, he sat back in the chair, sliding the ice pick under the back of his right leg. He picked up his glass with his left hand and drained the last remaining lemonade.

"Mind if I have some more?" he asked. She turned to see him holding out the glass.

"Not at all," she said, taking the glass from his hand and walking to the icebox.

She bent slightly and opened the door and, without looking, searched the top of the icebox with her fingers. Feeling around blindly, she began to stand straight when she felt his hand clamp hard around her mouth, splitting her bottom lip with the force. A muffled cry turned to a whimper as she tasted a mix of blood and axle grease. The ice pick's sharp point against her jugular needed little pressure and she froze, petrified with fear.

"Upstairs," he said. His stinking breath pushed its way into her nostrils.

She wanted to struggle, but the fear she felt and the look in his eyes told her better. Stiff legged, she moved up the stairs, his hand still tight over her mouth and the sharpness of the ice pick pushing just under her jaw line. He held her as he kicked the door to her bedroom open and flung her like a rag doll onto the bed.

"One word bitch and you die," he said, his eyes cutting through her. He waved the ice pick in the air punctuating his point. She looked up at him. Sweat dripped off the end of his twisted nose. She saw his fist and then an explosion of white light. She woke to a hazy, smoke filled house, smelling of burned pork.

Her swollen right eye throbbed as she struggled to rise from the bed and stopped. Afraid, she listened carefully. Was he still in the house? She looked down on the floor at her torn dress and undergarments. Groaning, she clutched her head with both hands and slid off the bed.

Painfully, she staggered to the bathroom and looked in the mirror. Her upper eyelid was a deep purple and the cheekbone welted red and was beginning to match the eyelid. Dried blood covered her split lip. Four sliding finger marks of grease painted her right cheek. The pain in her face did not match that of what she felt between her thighs. She turned to the commode and lowered herself to her knees.

Her loud heaving blocked out the sounds of her Aunt and Uncle coming into the house and opening windows. A far away voice called her name. Her throat felt tight and constricted as if his hand still gripped it. She gasped and spun when a hand touched her shoulder. Phyllis screamed for Jim. He came running up the stairs and stopped short at the closed bathroom door. Phyllis wrapped a towel around Nellie's shivering naked body.

"What is it?" he said.

"It's Nellie, Jim," she answered. The bathroom door opened.

Jim stepped inside and saw his niece seated on the floor, wrapped in the towel, rocking back and forth. Phyllis knelt beside her.

"Who did this to you?" Jim said. His fiery eyes searched around the bathroom as if the assailant was in the room.

"WHO, I SAID!" His voice boomed.

Nellie swallowed trying to make her sore throat work. She whispered to him.

"Nate."

She turned her head into Phyllis's shoulder and sobbed. Phyllis held her tight and stroked her hair.

Jim turned on his heels and ran down the steps. They heard the glass in the front door shatter when he slammed the door. He ran to the guesthouse. The door was open wide. He reached into the pocket of his pants and pulled out the pistol he carried while at the restaurant. The room with the bed in it was empty. Quietly, he walked through the small guesthouse and workshop. A dirty door hid the workshop and he kicked at it, cracking the frame. He kicked it one more time and the door gave way, showering splinters down on him. He thrust the two shot derringer out in front of him and looked around. The place was empty.

* * *

Nate Martin went from one speakeasy to the next, drinking everything he could get his hands on. He gulped bourbon and corn liquor, beer, and wine; anything that came in a glass or bottle. By the time he left his last stop, he was almost incoherent. He staggered blindly out the door and crossed the street. He weaved and grabbed onto a light pole as he stumbled to the other side.

Drunkenly, he looked around trying to get his bearings. He couldn't remember where he was as he sidled up the walk and turned down into an alley that led to the tracks used by the New York Central. He followed the dirt path that led up to the tracks and slipped on the chunky gravel used as the bed for the track. Tripping on his shoelace, he crawled on his hands and knees until he reached the top.

He cursed his luck and swore into the air. He bent down to tie the lace that had made him stumble and fall in the first place. The smell of the creosote from the wooden ties combined with all the alcohol made his head spin. The tracks spun crazily like some giant pinwheel. He gagged and threw up onto the ties, some of it landing on his boots. He leaned back with a lace in each hand, pulling himself off balance and landing on the seat of his pants.

The six-fifteen passenger train from Richmond was punctual as usual. The train bore down on him, the engineer hard on the throttle. By the time the engineer realized he was looking at Martin's back, fifteen cars had chewed him to shreds, twelve more continued over what remained. Only then did the brakes catch and halt the train. What little was left of Nate Martin could have easily fit in a coal bucket, with room for a few shovels of coal.

* * *

Aunt Phyllis nursed Nellie back from the physical pain, but the mental damage was going to be long lasting. She rarely left her room, and only to come down to make a cup of tea. Her uncle and aunt tried to make sure at least one of them could be there for her. In the kitchen, she couldn't bring herself to look out the window by the sink. It had been three weeks since the rape. Her cheek was turning a blue-green and her eyelid still had a purple color to it like a concord grape. Her voice had returned.

Two more weeks passed and her monthly never arrived. Six mornings she awoke nauseous and ran to the commode. One morning she hung onto the water closet of the commode, retching and gasping for air. She hoisted herself up and stood staring into the mirror. The only evidence from the attack left on her face was a brownish red clot in her right eye by the tear duct. Nellie was scared, not wanting to tell anyone, especially her mother. She had begged Phyllis not to tell her mother about the rape, mainly for the shame she felt.

One morning after her uncle went to work and she finished throwing up, she went downstairs. Aunt Phyllis was sitting at the drop leaf table drinking a cup of coffee. Nellie slid out a chair and sat down.

"Good morning," Nellie said.

"Hello honey," Phyllis said. "You're looking much better."

"I feel better," she lied. "My eye is almost healed completely."

"Nellie?" Phyllis said, "I heard you the last few mornings in the bathroom. Did you have your monthly?"

Nellie thought for a minute, but didn't want to hesitate for fear of giving herself away. She just knew she looked guilty and she felt her face growing hot. Nellie wasn't good at lying. She had relationships with her relatives that just didn't require it.

"Uh yes, I finished last week," Nellie replied. "Could I see the society section?" She wanted the subject changed as quickly as possible.

Phyllis removed the section and handed it to Nellie, paying particular attention to her shaking hands, but saying nothing more. She had her suspicions and prayed she was wrong. Nellie had never lied and she didn't think she ever would. She watched her as she read the paper for a moment, and then went back to her reading.

* * *

Four months later Nellie stood in the bathroom, lifting up her big skirt and noticing her swollen belly. She thought she had felt movement for a few weeks and now she no longer doubted the fact: She was pregnant. She had let out the seams of all her skirts to hide it and was working at the restaurant just as hard as she did before. She still attended classes, and did well, although her concentration often shifted from the business world to the baby world.

She sat in her room thinking of how she would tell Aunt Phyllis. She would understand, she thought. However, her mother concerned her most. She would have to know everything: Know how it happened and why she hadn't told her before. God, she thought, what can I do? She covered her face with her hands and sobbed. I have to tell them, she thought. It's driving me crazy.

She thought of leaving, maybe writing a note and then, with the money she saved, moving to Wheeling or maybe Pittsburgh. She agonized over it daily. She even considered going to that doctor, the one who had his office in the alley just off Lewis Street. It was illegal, but for the fifty dollars he charged, what did he care. Who would he tell anyway? The ones that did end up with an infection or plain hemorrhaged in his office, well, he always got his payment in advance. She became pre-occupied with it, even leaving the money meant for the safe on Uncle Jim's desk one night.

During the fifth month, Nellie decided to tell her aunt. She yelled from the top of the stairs and waited.

"Coming," Phyllis said, her voice carrying upstairs.

Nellie walked into her room and took a seat on the edge of her bed.

"What is it dear?" Phyllis said tenderly as she pulled out the desk chair and sat down.

"I lied."

"What? About what?" Phyllis asked.

"Well, you know what happened to me in the beginning of June," she swallowed hard. Her sweating palms tingled, and she suddenly felt very warm. There was just no easy way to put it. She looked at her Aunt and blurted out her secret.

"I'm going to have that man's baby."

"Oh, Nellie," she said, getting up from the desk and moving to the bed. She wrapped her arms around her shoulders. Nellie pulled away, feeling ashamed and unclean.

"I had to lie. I was so afraid. I didn't know what to do." She sat straight and looked into her aunt's eyes. "You'll never believe me again, will you?"

"Sure, I will. It's not your fault at all." Phyllis took both of Nellie's hands in hers. "Did you tell your mother?"

"No, nothing. I didn't want to upset her or make her worry about me. It will kill her," Nellie said, tightening the grip on her aunt's hands. "What should I do? What?"

"We need to let her know. You know that," Phyllis said.

"I know," Nellie agreed. Her shoulders slumped and she hung her head.

"Your mama loves you too much to let anything come between the two of you," she reassured her and added, "Don't worry; I'll talk to her first."

"Oh, Aunt Phyllis," Nellie said, her voice cracking.

Phyllis held her as the tears spilled down her cheeks. She rocked her gently, wondering how Anna would take the news.

* * *

The beginning of March did not roar like a lion, instead it brought labor pains and groans from Nellie's place on the bed. Nellie's mother arrived the night before and the Reeves hired an Amish midwife. They brought her all the way down from Lancaster, Pennsylvania. They would keep it as quiet as possible and hidden. Nellie had graduated from the business school and interviewed with a glass factory. An unwed mother would never find work in the kind of position she wanted.

Nellie gripped the corners of the blanket with one hand and bit down hard. The midwife placed towels underneath her and Anna sat in a chair holding her daughter's hand. The midwife stood over her and told her to breathe. Aunt Phyllis stayed until Nellie began to scream and then left the room. She wished she could help, but couldn't stand the sound of her niece screaming in pain.

Nellie felt the contractions and listened to the instructions of the heavy-set Amish woman. She spoke with a heavy German accent and, even with the pain she felt, Nellie would grimace and smile.

"Outten the lights," the midwife said, pointing to the window shade and looking at Anna.

Anna let go of Nellie's grip and pulled the shades down to hide the morning sunlight. Anna quickly sat back down and sponged the sweat from Nellie's forehead with a washcloth.

"Poosh it hard down. Voman. It von't hurt more." The midwife bent over and saw that Nellie was beginning to crown.

"I'm am...pushing...!" Nellie said through clenched teeth. She squeezed Anna's hand.

"Poosh."

Nellie screamed loud. She pushed again and the baby's head was in sight.

"Von time more. Poosh!"

Nellie bore down with her last ounce of strength and then she heard the cry.

The midwife held the baby, cut and tied the umbilical cord with all the precision of an expert. She carried the baby over to a pitcher and basin that was setting on a dry sink and cleaned the newborn up. She wrapped it in a small soft blanket and presented it to Nellie. The mid-wife remained iron faced as she put the baby on Nellie's wavering stomach.

"It's a girl," she said, looking at Nellie for just a second and getting back to her duties as simply as if she had been baking bread. Nellie cried when she looked at the tiny human on her stomach. Her mother wiped away the tears and called for Phyllis. She came into the room with a potted lily, smiling broadly, her hands trembling as she set the pot on a stand near Nellie.

"It's a girl, auntie," Nellie said, drained and happy it was all over. The two women hovered over the newborn. They checked toes, fingers, and remarked about the hair color. Finally, they agreed that Nellie had to rest.

Anna kissed her daughter on the cheek and the two women left, leaving the midwife to clean up. Nellie looked at the card on the lily pot, "To mother and baby. Love, Uncle Jim."

THIRTEEN
SUN DROPS AND STOCK DROPS

Nellie sat on the chair in the lobby of the Owens Glass Company. She wore a brown tweed business suit. The skirt was mid-calf, and she had her blonde hair bobbed. She wore a string of pearls and a brown cloche pulled down so that her eyes just peeked out from underneath. She had a clutch purse in her hand and a leather portfolio containing recommendations from some very influential people in Charleston.

Nellie watched as the receptionist answered the telephone and scribbled messages on a pad. As she waited, she took out a plastic tortoise shell case, opened it, and double-checked her frugal make up. She smoothed down her skirt and folded her hands in her lap. Nervous, she looked around the lobby to ease her mind. Different types of glass set against the walls: plate glass and several different types of window glasses. A huge oil painting of the founder hung on the wall. His eyes seemed to follow her.

"Mrs. Bell, or is it Miss?" the receptionist asked.

"I'm widowed," Nellie replied, unconsciously picking at the seam of her skirt.

"Oh, I see," the receptionist said, looking embarrassed. "Mr. Owens will see you now." She pointed to a massive oak door, deeply grained, and polished to a high luster. The huge brass knob shined, making Nellie's reflection look like she was peering into a fun house mirror. She knocked on the door.

"Come in," a voice from the other side answered. She opened the door and stepped inside, seeing a silver haired man in his early fifties. He wore a white dress shirt, suspenders, and a crooked red bow tie.

"Have a seat," the superintendent said motioning toward a leather chair.

The chair squeaked when she sat facing the huge credenza. She folded her hands on her lap.

"I'm Boscar Owens, the superintendent for Owen Glass," he said with little emotion.

He tapped his finger on the top of the desk and then reached toward a lacquered humidor. Choosing one, he closed the lid with a soft click. Like small bellows, he noisily sucked the flame from a lighter to the cigar.

"Now, Mrs. Bell," he said, exhaling a white cloud of smoke. "I've gone over your resume and, honestly, I am quite impressed." He rolled the cigar between his thumb and forefinger.

"Thank you, Mr. Owens," she replied.

"The references you supplied me with are impressive as well," he said, taking another long draw on the cigar. "Your uncle's restaurant seems to be doing quite well under your guidance, and the food isn't bad either. I've been in there a few times." He leaned back in the chair and closed his eyes. Nellie watched him and waited anxiously for him to speak. She couldn't remember ever meeting someone who took so long in thought before they spoke. She shifted in her chair, feeling uncomfortable.

"I need some help in marketing a new product. The position is basically in house. I need some heavy advertising and I need someone who can efficiently set up contacts for potential clients, sort of get our foot in the door before the sales staff meets them face to face." He opened his eyes and leaned forward.

"Do you think you could handle such a position?" he said, putting the cigar in the ashtray and standing up. He stretched and walked to a wooden cabinet tight against the wall. Opening the door, he took out a cut glass decanter.

Her eyes moved, following him, until she finally had to swing around in her chair just to make sure she could address him. They never taught this kind of interview technique in school. It was extremely casual, she thought.

"Yes sir, I believe that I could handle it without any problem," she said, reaching down to her side and lifting up her portfolio. "Would you like to see my portfolio?" she added.

He twisted the lid of the decanter of illegal scotch back on and lifted the glass to his mouth, sipping and then motioning with his hand, waving off the offer of the portfolio.

"Not necessary," he said. "I've heard nothing but good things about you; I did a little checking up myself."

Nellie was beginning to worry. What did he mean by that? If he knew she was an unwed mother, her chance for the job would end right there.

"Sir, I ah..." she started to say.

He interrupted her.

"I understand you're widowed. I'm very sorry and it has to be difficult raising a daughter whose Daddy died in France." She looked at him as he walked around to his desk and sat down. "Can you start on Monday?" the superintendent said, picking up the cigar and relighting it. His eyes looked out from under raised eyebrows.

"Yes sir, "Nellie said.

"Good, good," he said. "Miss Lyons, the receptionist, will show you your office and will fill you in on the other details. Thank you for coming in," he said, rising from the desk and extending his hand. Nellie shook his hand and thanked him. The receptionist spent another hour taking her around the plant and showing her the office that would be hers.

"Aunt Phyllis, Aunt Phyllis," Nellie called through the house in a happy voice.

"Up here, dear." she answered from upstairs in the room they had turned into a nursery.

Nellie ran up the steps, her soles tapping all the way. She ran into the nursery and picked up Barbara from her crib. Holding her close and spinning in one big circle, she kissed the baby's face.

"I got it, Aunt Phyllis, I start on Monday. I even have an office," Nellie said, shrilling with the excitement.

"Wonderful," said Phyllis, standing up from the rocking chair and hugging her. Phyllis moved to a seat on the cushioned top of a hope chest.

Nellie sat in the rocking chair. She rocked the baby and stroked her hair.

"Did you miss Mommy, today?" Nellie said, in a near whisper. Barbara Bell was truly her own little bundle of joy, whenever Phyllis and Jim weren't hovering over her.

Phyllis looked at the pendulum clock hanging on the wall of the nursery and quickly got up from the cedar hope chest. "I didn't realize it was so late. Jim will be home and I haven't started a thing for supper."

"Would you like some help?" Nellie asked.

"No, it's feeding time for Barbara, so take care of that and I'll feed the other big baby."

They both laughed at the remark. Phyllis left to go downstairs and Nellie stayed to spend some time alone with her child. She had worked at the restaurant the last few weeks, teaching Jim how to run things in the office. Phyllis spent very little time at the business. She was just having the time of her life baby-sitting seven-month-old Barbara.

Nellie looked down into the face of her baby. Everyone said she looked just like her when she was a baby. Nellie studied little Barbara's face and then down to her hands and looked at her fingers. She moved back up and intently looked again at her face. She has my nose and blue eyes, she thought. She hoped that the baby wouldn't have any of the features of Nate Martin. Barbara was enough of a daily reminder of him as it stood.

Nellie fed her daughter and changed the cloth diapers, carrying the heavy diaper pail downstairs and washing them in the laundry room. She hated scrubbing the diapers and then pinning them up on the clothesline that stretched across the small room in the back of the house. She wondered how her child could go through so many. She finished pinning up the last diaper and went into the parlor to find Aunt Phyllis sitting on the couch knitting yet another blanket.

"She's going to have more blankets than she'll know what to do with," Nellie said.

"You know how cold it can get here. I don't think you could ever have too many," Phyllis said with the concern of a doting mother.

Nellie turned on the radio and the two of them listened to a broadcast out of Pittsburgh. It was hard to hear. They had to have just the right weather to listen to KDKA, and that was usually when it rained. It wouldn't be until 1926 that Charleston would have its own radio station. They listened to the static sounding voice of the announcer until it just wasn't worth the bother and she shut it off.

* * *

Nellie performed her job at the glass plant so well that they put her in charge of four men and two other women who contacted customers. The sales increased throughout the southern region and there was even talk of expanding into the Midwest. She promoted all the new products, increasing the customer base by thirty percent. An additional seventy men became new employees. The plant went public and offered shares of stock in order to open another plant in Cincinnati, Ohio.

Nellie bought a 1923 Buick, straight eight. It was canary yellow and she had Uncle Jim teach her how to drive it. The first few times the car bucked and stalled as she tried shifting. She would let the clutch out so fast with her foot heavy on the accelerator, snapping her uncle's head back and causing his fedora to end up in the back seat. Finally, she managed to work out the details so she had enough time and money to spend a weekend back in Oak Hill with her mother.

* * *

The Buick bounced along the road and Nellie hung onto the steering wheel, feeling it jerk each time one of the big wheels dipped in a pothole. Barbara was sleeping in the back seat and the bouncing of the auto didn't seem to bother her at all. They passed over the Gauley Bridge and Nellie stared straight ahead. The height bothered her as she anticipated reaching the other side. She exhaled a sigh of relief when she felt the Buick's rear tires bump as they left the bridge surface.

She pulled up in front of the house, the front tire going up on the curb and then bouncing down with just enough force to wake up four-year-old Barbara. Frankie and Anna were expecting them and were waiting in the front yard. Frankie shook his head as he watched Nellie's driving skills. Nellie walked around to the passenger side of the car, just in time to catch Barbara, who had started to climb over the front seat and tumbled headlong into her mother's arms.

Nellie and Anna spent the night catching up on all the news of Nellie's job and the success of the restaurant. Anna had given up the boarding business and they were living comfortably on the money Frankie earned in the mines. On Sunday, the four of them went to church. Nellie offered to drive them and, with a little resistance from Frankie, they finally agreed.

After church, Nellie and Anna cooked an early Sunday dinner with fried chicken and all the fixings. While they cooked, Frankie played with Barbara in the parlor. She was practicing her ABC's that Nellie had taught her. They ate and Nellie helped her mother in the kitchen with the dishes. Barbara slept soundly on a blanket on the floor of the dining room.

"I'm so happy for you," Anna said. She dried a dish and put it up in the cupboard.

"Things are going very well. I'm thinking about renting an apartment. Uncle Jim and Aunt Phyllis have been so helpful; I wouldn't know how to ever repay them. They treat Barbara like she's their own daughter," Nellie said as she scrubbed the big pot with a chunk of steel wool.

"They're very special people. My sister and I've never had a cross word that I can remember," Anna said.

"They probably won't want me to leave now, but I'm ready to get my own place. I'm making almost three thousand dollars a year now, and I can afford it. I may just rent a house," Nellie said.

"Well, I think you'll do just fine. It looks to me like you've accomplished a lot in the last four years. Have you met anyone yet? You know... a man?" Anna asked. She didn't want to sound too nosey or pushy. She put a dish in the cupboard and quickly glanced at Nellie, trying to read her reaction.

"No mother, I haven't. I really don't have the time with work and Barbara," Nellie said, not showing any hint of regret.

"Oh, I just wondered," Anna said as she took the pot from Nellie's hands and dried it. She set the bottom of the heavy pot up on the sink and tilted it toward her, drying the inside.

"I know you think I probably hate men, don't you." Nellie said softly. "I mean with everything that has happened, and with Cotton. Well, I don't. I just have a life that keeps me pretty busy, and it's not all that easy to find someone who wants a ready-made family."

"No, no, I didn't mean anything like that, honey." Anna said, apologetically. She wished she could change the subject.

"I know, Mama, it's just that sometimes I feel like I might end up being an old maid, and it bothers me, you know?" Nellie said, "I have time, Mama. I'm only twenty-six."

"Beautiful, too," Anna replied, smiling. She reached up and took Nellie's face in her hands. "I love you and whatever your choices are, nothing will ever change between us. You gave me a beautiful little granddaughter. I count my blessings."

"I love you too, Mama. You raised me the best anyone ever could and I hope that I can do the same for Barbara," Nellie said, a tear spilling down her cheek.

"I hope she turns out just like you," Anna said.

They finished the dishes and Nellie planned to drive back to Charleston. She had never driven back from Oak Hill after dark and she gathered up her things for the trip back. Her mother gave her some leftover fried chicken to take with her, and some clothes that she bought for Barbara at the company store. They pulled away with Barbara waving happily from the front seat.

In May, Nellie found a house. The fifty dollars a month rent was reasonable and, with six rooms, she would have more than enough space. It was on the outskirts of town, close to the glass plant, and would be near the small private country school that Barbara would be starting in September. She didn't want her going to the school in the city. She really thought that she needed more attention and could get that at the smaller school.

Nellie noticed things about Barbara. She seemed to be changing and she thought the attention she would receive at the school would help. A woman by the name of Henrietta agreed to baby-sit for the few hours before Nellie finished work during the week. She had answered her ad in the city paper and the woman seemed very nice. She lived close enough, too. She would walk to the school, pick up Barbara, and stay with her at the new house until Nellie got home.

Nellie walked across the field, with Barbara's tiny hand in hers. It was the first day of school. She had her lunch pail in her hand, swinging it as Nellie looked down at her. She had beautiful blonde hair that hung in big curls, and a little nose. She looks almost like I used to, Nellie thought. The only difference was the eyes. They were blue at birth but took on the gray color of Nate Martin. There was something deeper and foreboding about her eyes though: Not during Barbara's happy moments, but when something didn't go her way. It was then that they flashed with anger. There were times when she would lash out; Nellie looked down at her own black and blue shins and remembered.

Nellie and Barbara cut through the back yard of the house and followed a footpath that went down through the woods and came out into another opening. They could see the quaint white building in the distance with its small bell tower that looked more like a church steeple. They stopped just at the wood line and saw some late blooming evening primrose. Nellie knew of them as "sun drops", because of their beautiful yellow color.

"Look at the pretty flowers. Want to take some to your teacher? It would be nice of you to do it," Nellie said, touching the soft yellow petals.

"Yeah, Mommy," she said, jumping up and down. "Can I pick them out?"

"Sure."

Nellie watched Barbara picking the flowers.

They walked across the field to the school. Barbara squeezed her hand tightly as they neared the steps. It reminded Nellie of her first day of school. The teacher was waiting outside on the porch and busying herself with introductions.

"Hello," she said with a kind soft voice. She stooped to make eye contact with Barbara. "Welcome to school. We're going to have a lot of fun."

Nellie looked at the young teacher. She couldn't have been anymore than twenty-two. She looked at Barbara for a reaction, but there was none. She just stared at the teacher. Nellie was familiar with that defensive gaze.

"Come with me and we'll get you started. You have a desk, and we're going to finger-paint today," the young teacher said.

Barbara looked up at Nellie with a trembling lip, "Mommy?"

"It will be fine. Did you show your teacher the flowers you picked for her?" Nellie looked at the teacher and smiled.

Barbara slowly held the bunch of flowers out and gave them to the teacher.

"Why, thank you. They're beautiful. Let's go find a vase and we'll put them in some water."

Barbara let go of Nellie's hand and the teacher turned with Barbara at her heels. Nellie watched them disappear into the school. She strolled across the field and stopped, plucking a sun drop for her flower book. She had made Barbara a book like her mother had made for her when she was born. She found it one day in the backyard, torn to shreds. Barbara had taken it outside hidden under her dress.

Barbara passed on to the second grade, but barely. Nellie let her stay with her mother for the summer with hopes she could do something to change the little girl's attitude. Anna told her she thought she was just spoiled and Nellie needed to be firmer with her.

The school offered but one more chance for a change in Barbara's behavior. They warned Nellie, if Barbara continued her disruptive ways, they would not hesitate to expel her. Nellie thought of taking her to a psychologist. Maybe it was something else, she thought. She wondered if Nate Martin lived inside her daughter. She prayed not. The first two months of the school year seemed to be better for Barbara, and Nellie was hoping the change was long lasting. She hired a patient woman from Charleston as her new sitter. Barbara appeared to like the woman, and did show some promising signs; however, she was a great manipulator.

Nellie knew also that the day would come for Barbara to ask the question she dreaded. The day came on a Saturday in early September. A hot day, with just enough of a breeze to dry the paint quickly on an old dresser Nellie was refinishing on the front porch of the house. Barbara ran up the steps onto the porch and plopped down on the slats of the old wooden swing. It creaked as she rocked it gently back and forth.

"Mama?" Barbara asked.

"Yes, dear." Nellie dabbed the thick paint on the stout leg of the dresser.

"Viola Simmons asked me why I don't have a Daddy."

Nellie stopped in mid-stroke of the brushing. She set the brush across the open can of paint and pushed herself up off her knees. Walking slowly toward the girl, she rehearsed what she practiced so many nights in her mind. Nellie sat beside her on the swing.

"Honey, your Daddy was in the war." Nellie said. She swallowed hard when Barbara turned her gray eyes up to meet hers. Nellie brushed a blond lock from her forehead.

"Your Daddy didn't come back from France, honey."

"Why not?"

"Daddy was killed in a big battle over there."

The swing creaked as Barbara's feet pushed off the boards of the porch, and it rocked gently. She stared at her feet, thinking.

"Was he a hero, Mommy?"

"There were lots of heroes over there."

Barbara fiddled with the rusted chain holding her side of the swing.

"Viola's Daddy wasn't even in any war, I bet." Barbara said.

"Well, I guess he's a lucky man."

Barbara jumped off the swing and hop scotched to the steps.

"I'm gonna go play now, "she said. She ran down the steps and disappeared around the corner of the house. Nellie heard her yelling to her playmate.

"Viola! Guess what? My Daddy was a hero." Nellie bent her head and covered her face with her hands.

* * *

It was near the end of October, and Nellie sat in the small living room of her house. Warm heat blew through the floor registers. Soft music drifted from the floor model radio, and Nellie relaxed on the couch with her feet propped on an ottoman. She sipped on a cup of tea.

She had been busy at work today and deliberated with a customer most of the morning over a wrong shipment. He had threatened to take his business elsewhere, but Nellie knew his account was one of the biggest. She set things right and by the time she finished on the phone with him, he had placed a new five thousand-dollar order. Mr. Owens took her to lunch over the deal.

She leaned her head back and closed her tired eyes when the music abruptly stopped. She half listened, not really paying attention to the fifteen seconds of dead air. She was used to it. Her eyes opened when she heard the frantic shuffling of papers and muffled voices of urgency in the background. The announcer cleared his throat.

Nellie sat up leaning in the direction of the speaker. The nervous announcer fumbled over the words and started again. The stock market dropped and sixteen million shares offered up for sale couldn't find a single buyer.

"My God," Nellie said. She spoke to the speakers as if they would answer back. She was wide-eyed and oblivious to everything except the announcer's voice. He went on to say that a number of suicides occurred and read some names. One was the man who had placed the five thousand dollar order that she wrote up earlier in the day. He had lost everything in the course of an eight-hour day on Wall Street.

FOURTEEN
THE LETTER

In the darkness of her room, Nellie listened to Mrs. Martz berating a student who just could not grasp the state capitals.

"Young man, you will learn these capitals whether you choose to or not. Now, one more time," Mrs. Martz said in a firm tone with the sound of her bedsprings squeaking. She was lifting her leg just off the bed and letting it fall with the rhythm of her quizzing. The bedsprings squeaked with her impatience for an answer

"Ohio. Very good," she praised the invisible student for answering correctly.

"Tennessee. Try again, young man. Tennessee," Praise followed a squeak of anticipation, "very good."

Nellie was in the mood for a little late night humor. She waited until Martz asked the next state, and then Nellie rolled on her stomach and placed her lips close to the wall. "Arkansas," Martz said and the bed springs bounced.

"Poughkeepsie," Nellie said lowering her voice gruffly.

"That is incorrect, son. Try again." Martz asked again in a commanding voice, "Arkansas?"

"Mars," Nellie said.

"It obvious you're playing games with me, son. Are you?"

"No ma'am," Nellie said, with a laugh escaping her lips, and her eyes watering with tears.

"Arkansas." The rattling bedsprings chirped.

"King Tutsville," Nellie said, laughing out loud.

The bedsprings rattled and Nellie thought Mrs. Martz would fall through the slats, mattress and all.

"You have just earned yourself a trip to the principal's office young man!" Martz yelled and Nellie pounded her fist on her mattress laughing and wiping tears from her eyes. Her ribs ached and finally she closed her eyes, the smile slow to leave her face.

In the morning, Nellie woke early as usual and took her bath. The walker gathered dust in the corner by the window. She hadn't used it for months. Her hip rarely ached with pain anymore.

Nellie found a tube of bright tangerine lipstick in the bottom of one of the drawers and put it on. She checked it in the mirror and picked up a tissue, pulling her lips in and gumming down on the paper. She looked at the perfectly formed set of lip prints. Elaina had brought her a tube of lip balm and her lips were no longer cracked. She walked briskly, with her shoulders back, to the dining room for breakfast.

She took a seat across from Banks, who shielded his plate with his forearm. He was not sure if she took his fish that day, but later he had sat in his room and took stock in his mind. Two hours after the fish dinner, the fact remained he was starving. Nellie looked at him with her lips pursed in a smooch and smacked a kiss his way.

"Mata Hari," he said smartly. He lifted his other arm, encircling the plate with both forearms, and his hands clasped in front of the plate.

As Nellie waited for her breakfast, she passed the time watching the activity. The round dining tables and the pastel colored plastic chairs with the uncomfortable curved bottoms made the place look like a kindergarten room. The lady with the bald patches on her hair lifted a glass of milk up to her wrinkled lips and Nellie watched as the cup shook, dumping the milk down the front of her already filthy flannel robe. The woman set the cup down. Her head slumped toward her chest, and she stared at the wet milk. With her fingers, she rubbed it in tiny circles and whimpered.

Nellie ate breakfast, threw one more kiss at Banks, and slid up from the chair. She ended up in the lounge. The big woman with the brown hair was sitting on the couch watching Looney Toons. She was laughing obnoxiously loud and stuffing bite-sized peanut butter cups in her mouth. Nellie turned her attention outside.

The parking lot was nearly empty with the exception of the few cars belonging to the staff. A white van with "Jimmy the Janitor" emblazoned on its sides pulled into the lot. She watched the man unload a big vacuum machine and then stepped out of his way when he came through the doors.

He rolled the machine behind the nurse's station. The loud, shrill machine failed to drown out the lady in the lounge. She threw her head back and howled with laughter. A pig's face came on the screen and she watched as it stuttered. It looked like the pig's head was sticking through a black tire or something. Nellie squinted to focus better. The black circle closed up and she couldn't see the pig's head anymore. The woman stomped her big foot on the carpeted floor with a heavy thud, disappointed that the cartoon was over.

Nellie shook her head and walked to her room. She closed her door and crawled into bed. She wrapped a pillow around her head, muffling the multitude of whining, talking, yelling, and screaming mayhem that was making her head pound. When she did finally fall asleep, she slept until well after noon.

Jimmy vacuumed around the chairs and the small square of carpet in the nurse's station. He put the suction head of the vacuum underneath the long console and watched as the balls of gray dust disappeared. A nurse walked through the door of the large cubicle and saw the man rolling up the hose on the vacuum.

"Could you please get under the copier? The service man said that dust wasn't any good for it," the nurse asked.

"Okay," he muttered, letting out a bored sigh as he unraveled the hose and tried to fit it under the big machine. He did not feel like moving it, but seeing it was on rollers, he dropped the hose on the floor with a clatter. The nurse gave him an angry look. He slid the heavy copier away from the wall, and picked up several dust covered letters, and a notepad. He tossed them all on the counter in front of the nurse. The startled nurse turned to look at him.

"Sorry," he said.

* * *

Nellie sat in the chair watching the sun creep down behind the parking lot. The tinged yellow and red of the maple leaves tattled of autumn. With the change of season came the heat inside the nursing home. It seemed at the first sign of cool weather someone would crank up the heat as if the patients were chicks in an incubator. She cooled her dry throat with a plastic cup of water. Exchanging her flower book for the cup, she heard the interrupting wheels of the med nurse's cart rolling toward her room.

Nellie took the pills tonight. She wanted a good night's sleep. Besides, she had stowed away enough of the sleeping pills that a little bulge was appearing on the back cover. She had plenty now. She only had to decide when to do the deed. Should she wait for her birthday? Maybe she would wait until next Mother's Day, which might leave Barbara one hell of a memory to carry around in life. The speedy effects of the pills led her to bed. She was sleeping in a matter of minutes.

She woke late in the morning, cursing.

"Damn those pills," she said groggily. She staggered to the bathroom. The cold water splashing on her face revived her some, but what she wanted was coffee, real honest to goodness coffee, not the watered down stuff they served. She dressed and arrived just in time to eat breakfast. Most of the others had finished a half-hour ago.

She finished eating and went back to her room, fiddling with her pocket on the way to make sure the three coffee packets she swiped and tucked in her pocket were still there. When she got to her room, she emptied all three into the plastic glass and filled it with hot tap water. She sat in her chair sipping on the coffee. It was bitter, but it worked to jumpstart her.

Elaina came into the room at eleven. She was whistling and had her hair braided with small red and blue beads.

"What are you so happy about?" Nellie said.

"Just happy is all."

"Could you spare some of it?" Nellie said curtly.

"I might be able to do that." Elaina stood with a hand on her hip and leaned toward Nellie.

"Oh come on, you've got enough joy in you for the both of us."

"Got something else too," she said as she tapped her small hand on the oversized pocket of her white smock.

"What ever could that be?" Nellie said, in her best Southern belle accent.

"Well, let's see, it's white and thin and it has your name on it," Elaina joked.

"A letter, now seriously don't be kidding me about that," Nellie said with searching eyes moving toward the pocket of Elaina's smock.

"We have a winner," Elaina said talking into a make believe microphone, clutched in her empty brown hand.

Elaina reached into the pocket of the smock and handed the letter to her. Nellie held it close to her eyes and then moved it back farther. Giving up on reading the small print, she handed it back to Elaina.

"I don't have my glasses. Read it to me, please."

Elaina looked at the return address and Nellie watched her thin black eyebrows rise.

"Come on now, girl. The suspense is killing me. I haven't received one letter since I've been in this hole in the wall," Nellie said.

Elaina opened the letter and sat on the edge of the bed. She scanned over it, quickly reading it to herself. Halfway through reading, she stopped and turned toward the open door. Nellie noticed that her hands were shaking.

"Miss Nellie, I'd better close the door." Elaina did not wait for her answer. She jumped up, stuck her head through the doorway, and checked up and down the empty halls. Nellie slid to the very edge of the chair with her forehead wrinkled in puzzlement. Elaina returned to Nellie's chair and lowered herself to her knees on the floor in front of her. She put her fingers up to her lips, motioning her to be very quiet.

She read the letterhead first, whispering. Her dark eyes darted from the letter to the door.

"It is from the Office of the Attorney General of West Virginia," she glanced at the door nervously. "It says a bunch of people filed a class action suit against a big coal company and a bank that's got a whole lot of offices all over the country. What they did was illegal. The bank and the coal company were taking coal that didn't belong to them. They were shuffling paperwork, changing names, and hiding payments. They did not have any right to the minerals underneath it, especially the way they went about doing it. A judge ruled in favor of the landowners and their survivors because they would have been able to make their payments by selling the coal that belonged to them in the first place."

She stopped talking when a pair of feet blocked the light coming in from underneath the door, hesitated, and then went on their way. She exhaled and read the rest of the letter.

"It says that you have a check waiting at the attorney general's office."

Elaina's eyes opened wide and her full lips formed into a pucker as she whistled softly.

"What?" Nellie said, responding to the whistle.

"Miss Nellie, the check is for more than...four-hundred- thousand dollars," Elaina looked down, reading it again. "Wait, wait, four-hundred- seventy-four thousand, and ninety-two dollars."

A muddling of happiness and fear coursed through Nellie. Elaina reached up and held her trembling hand. Nellie leaned her head back and closed her eyes, tears flowing down her cheeks. Whom could she trust? If Barbara got wind of this, she would be there in no time at all.

The only person she felt could help her, and whom she could entrust the matter to, was in front of her.

"Elaina," she said, trying to catch her breath, "I need your help. Find me the best lawyer in Dallas. No, wait. West Virginia. The way those crooks talk among themselves, Barbara's lard ass husband would be sure to get wind of it, and they'd find some way of keeping me in here. I'm getting the hell out of this place. Take the letter with you and when you get home, make a copy of it. That way the lawyer won't doubt that I can afford to pay for his services. Better yet, I want a woman lawyer. I know one up in Charleston: Bonnie Kay Galloway. She's the best in West Virginia. I've known her since grade school."

"I will, Miss Nellie. Don't you worry and don't tell a soul in here. They would love to get their hands on your money. Hell, they suck up these old folk's social security like it is their own. The administrator would have a field day with yours," Elaina said, serious and still whispering. She got up from the floor and slid the envelope and letter into her pocket.

"See ya later, Nellie," Elaina said.

"Bye, sweetheart."

Elaina opened the door and stuck her head out, checking. She pinched her thumb and forefinger together giving Nellie the all-clear sign behind her back and left. Nellie heard her whistling as she went down the hall as if it was just another night. Her whistling garnered attention from Banks.

"Viva La France," yelled Banks.

Nellie tossed back her head and laughed hard.

"Yes, Viva La France," she said, "and Viva La Moi."

Miracles do happen, Nellie thought. She knew she would need a bigger miracle than just money. The amount of money sounded great, but what use would it be to her if she had to stay here? It would be worthless, she thought. She needed more, not just the damn money. She needed Barbara out of her life, which she desperately wanted back. Barbara did not have to visit; she did not have to be anywhere close to her to wield her control. She had the power and Nellie had to find a way to remove the hold she had on her. Somehow, Barbara was managing to snatch the joy of the letter away, even though she was miles from here.

Nellie rose from her chair and returned with her book. She opened it to a page that brought back memories of soup lines and hard times. The Depression years that she had managed to survive built her strength. The strength she would once again have to summon to defeat Barbara. She opened the book.

Taped to a page was a small brown wrinkled bag. Inside it, the seeds of hollyhocks and, beside it, a sketched picture of one of the tall plants she had drawn so many years ago. She looked at the drawing and noticed the lines of the fence behind the plant. A closer look revealed to her the fence that once bordered her Mother's yard.

FIFTEEN
HOLLYHOCKS AND HUNGER

The Great Depression took some time to get rolling, but when it did its waves ripped through the mountains and valleys of West Virginia like a tsunami. The path of destruction it left in its wake cost jobs, businesses, and, in some cases, even lives. People tried to outrun it by heading west to the "land of opportunity", only to end up in choking dust that drifted high enough to nearly cover houses. The migration from East to West, from the Rust Bowl to the Dust Bowl, left people exchanging their wooden miner shacks for shanties constructed of old Kotex cartons and tin, wall papered inside with layers of Post Toasties boxes.

* * *

"You need to see me?" Nellie asked, standing in front of Mr. Owens' desk. His usually happy face looked drawn, tired, and deep worry lines appeared almost overnight. The clothes were the same as he wore yesterday, and his fragrant aftershave smelled like old booze to her.

"Yes, Nellie, please...please have a seat," he said, extending his hand with his trembling palm up and motioning to the chair behind her.

She sat with her hands folded on her lap. He cleared his throat and ran his fingers through his uncombed gray hair.

"I don't know an easy way to put this," he said, "I guess there really isn't one." The nail of his pinky clicked against the wood of the desk. "We're closing," he said. His bloodshot eyes grew sadder with the tears.

"What?" Nellie said. Fear tightened her muscles and she sat up erect.

"The company stock is worthless and orders are just not coming in. It's like the whole country is broke." He rubbed his temples with two fingers of each hand.

"But what about all the back orders? That has to be worth something to keep us afloat?" she asked, quickly.

"Cancelled."

"They're obligated to buy. They contracted with us," Nellie said. She fidgeted in the seat.

"Worthless contracts, Nellie. You can't get blood from a turnip. Besides, we couldn't fill them. Our vendors are dropping like flies. We cannot get the raw materials. To make matters worse, Nellie, the banks collapsed yesterday. Their doors are locked. I can't borrow two cents."

He hung his head, "I'm sorry." His watery eyes focused on the desktop as she rose from the chair. She never offered him her hand, and the closing door behind her punctuated the silent goodbye. She cleared out her desk and walked to the Buick, her memories of Owens Glass rattling in a cardboard box.

For weeks, Nellie's search for work was fruitless. One day, she answered the loud knocking on the front door. The landlord greeted her with a hammer and a cardboard sign in his hands.

"I can't wait any longer for my rent. I have been patient for as long as I possibly can be, but a man has to eat too. Do you have it? You're three months back now," he said.

"Mr. Rowls, I told you I haven't been able to get my money out of the bank. They're all closed up. You know that," she said. She fought to control her growing temper with the thin, bearded man dressed in a cheap gray suit.

"Wouldn't matter, you lost your money. You're smart enough to know that, or don't you read the papers," he said sarcastically. He turned over the cardboard and painted on the sign in bright red paint dripped the words, "NO TRESPASSING."

"But...but," Nellie stammered with embarrassment and anger combined.

"No buts to it. I want you out and I want you out by tomorrow morning or you can deal with Sheriff McQuire." He said something else but all she could hear was the pounding of the hammer as he nailed the cardboard to the side of the house. She slammed the door and leaned back against it weeping.

"Oh, and one last thing," he shouted through the door as soon as she heard the last whack of the hammer. "Don't take any of your furniture or appliances. They're mine until you pay up. Or you and your daughter will have a roof over your heads down at the county jail." She heard him clomp off the porch and then the sound of his Cadillac's wheels crunching the gravel as he backed up and drove off.

Nine-year-old Barbara came downstairs, saw her mother standing by the door, and watched as she dropped her hands from her tear stained face. "I suppose we'll have to go live with Grammy now. I hate that little town. There's never anything to do."

"Go to bed," Nellie screamed.

"I hate you, I hate you, I hate you," Barbara yelled, her face red with rage. She stomped up the stairs, her long curls bouncing with each hard step. Nellie walked into the parlor and slumped in her chair. She cried until she fell asleep.

The song of a whippoorwill woke Nellie up to a gray drizzling dawn. She got up from the chair and opened the door. The sign, still nailed to the side of the house, took away her hope that it all was just a bad dream. Nellie called her mother, told her of the situation, and then began the process of moving back to Oak Hill.

She had the phone disconnected and went through the house getting together the few things she would be able to fit inside the Buick. Barbara woke up and Nellie fixed her some rolled oats and honey.

While the girl ate, Nellie stepped outside onto the porch. The rain pattered on the roof and dripped from the eaves in long lines. She looked out toward Charleston. The stacks of the glass plant reached toward the gray sky. They were now devoid of the steam that once drifted out and hung lazily over the river.

She listened for the sounds of the once bustling industries and, try as she might, she could hear little activity. A faint whistling in the distance of a single coal barge, slowly making its way up the river, wailed mournfully. She looked out once more, toward downtown Charleston. She did not know if she had just joined the city in being a victim, or if the city had just joined her.

Nellie and Barbara packed clothes in boxes and carried the heavy contents to the car. Wet clods of sticky clay percolated through the thin layer of gravel and stuck to her shoes, adding more weight to an already overburdened body. She put the last box of silverware and dishes in the car.

There was just enough room for Barbara to sit in the front seat on a pile of blankets, leaving her head inches from the roof. The cold, gray March weather did little to lift her spirits as Nellie backed the Buick down the muddy driveway. The bumper of the auto scraped the pavement when she came up out of a dip and onto the main road. The Buick rode low, its springs compressed with the weight of the packed trunks in the back. She pointed the auto in the direction of Oak Hill and drove through the downpour, leaving a dying Charleston behind.

* * *

Frankie unloaded her things while Anna helped her out of her soaking clothes. Anna ran a hot bath and Nellie tried to soak the chill from her body. She still shivered when she finished. Barbara had remained dry during the move, helping pack things in the house, but refusing to carry anything to the car. She had sat in the parlor on the settee with her arms crossed and with her bottom lip curled in a pout.

Nellie slowly walked down the stairs, dressed in a cotton robe. Her mother wrapped a heavy gray wool blanket around her shoulders, and handed her a cup of steaming tea. The teacup shook in her hand, from both nerves and the cold that had seemed to penetrate her very bones.

"It's nice to have you back," Anna said, her gray hair pulled up in a bun and crow's feet radiating at the corners of her fading blue eyes. She patted Nellie's knee.

"I'm glad to be home too, Mother," Nellie said. She couldn't seem to get warm. Her teeth chattered and she said, "I need to get Barbara into school tomorrow."

Barbara's welfare always came first with Nellie, but she finally had to admit to herself that the circumstances of Barbara's conception resulted in her failing to discipline the child. She always felt guilty for not being tougher on her daughter, but the guilt of the rape weighed more. Barbara had an innate sense of Nellie's weakness and fed on it.

"Well, that won't be a problem. I'll go with you if you want," Anna offered.

"I'd like that very much, she's been a real handful the last few years," Nellie said, turning her eyes in the direction of the parlor and speaking low.

"Do you mind keeping an eye on her? I'm so tired, and if I could just lay down for awhile I'm sure I'd feel better," Nellie said softly. It seemed as if every fiber of her body ached.

"Go right ahead, I'll keep her occupied," Anna said. "Your old room is just the way you left it. I put clean bedding on it this morning."

Nellie rose weakly from the table. She stumbled and grabbed the back of the chair for support. Feeling dizzy, she painfully walked up the steps and crawled into her bed. Her body shivered even with three blankets and the feather tick mattress. She looked out the window and watched the rain through burning eyes. When she did finally drift off to sleep, it was for the entire night.

Anna made up a room for Barbara upstairs across the narrow hall from Nellie's room. It used to be the Irishman's room when she ran the boardinghouse. She was planning to do it again, since times were so hard. Anna showed Barbara the room and she looked around at it.

"Thank you, Grammy," she said. "I really like it.

"Well, you better get into bed because tomorrow you are going to the new school they built. It even has a gymnasium," Anna said.

Barbara crawled up in the bed and Anna pulled the blankets up underneath her chin. She kissed her on the forehead and switched off the light. "Good night," she said, turning and looking in on her one last time.

"Good night, Grammy." Barbara smiled at her.

Anna wondered why Nellie had so many problems with her. Anna shook her head, thinking that her daughter might be exaggerating about Barbara's behavior. She walked downstairs and into the kitchen. The heavy cookie jar sat on the new electric refrigerator and Anna lifted it down carefully. She dumped the contents and counted the money she saved, writing the amount on a scrap of paper. Nearly sixty dollars filled the jar. They would have a nice Christmas this year, she thought.

Anna waited up for Frankie to return home from the mines. He had been working late every night. At midnight she heard him entering the outside door to the cellar. Water sprayed from the new shower he had installed in the basement. She walked down the steps with a towel in her hand. A cloud of steam rolled from under the canvas tarp serving as a curtain. She bent down and picked up the heavy miner's belt he had dropped on the rough cemented floor and hung it up on a nail sticking out from a wooden support beam.

"Is that you, sweetheart?" he said, his eyes shut tightly and the lather covering his face.

"Yes, it is only me." She picked up the coal-dusted coveralls laying them on a wooden bench leaning crooked against the fieldstone wall of the basement.

"Hungry?" she asked.

"Starved," he replied, the sound of the hog bristle brush scouring away the dust resonated from behind the curtain.

"There's some potato soup left over. I'll warm it up for you."

"That's good."

The water slowed and stopped with a screech coming from the turning of the water valve, and she saw his hand reaching blindly for a towel. She reached up and lifted the towel off the spike, suddenly feeling his strong hand wrap around her wrist. Laughing, she fought his grip. The canvas rustled as her clothing flew over the space between the ceiling and the thick wire holding the makeshift curtain. He reached up turning the handle of the shower and the rush of water drowned the passionate noises coming from behind the wall of canvas.

* * *

Two weeks after her return home, Nellie's bout with pneumonia was over. Anna and Nellie worked in the kitchen making homemade noodles. Nellie rolled the dough out on the top of the wooden table. The heavy wooden rolling pin clunked as she flattened the dough. She scooped up flour from the tin, dusting it. The legs of the big table shook as she bore her weight down, transforming the dough into a tire-sized circle.

Her mother moved about the kitchen covering every available chair with clean white bed sheets. Two chairs already held two of the draping white circles of thin dough.

"There, all done," Nellie said. She slid her forearm across her perspiring forehead. The edges of the white bandanna tied on her head were wet with sweat. She stepped back from the table and Anna slid a hand under the edges of the dough, picking it up carefully and gently draping it over the clean sheet.

"This ought to last a few days," Anna said. With her hands on her hips, she eyed the dough with a furrowed brow. "We only have two boarders, but they eat like four."

Nellie pinched one of the circles of dough hanging on the back of a chair. "This one's dry already," she said. "I had best get cutting."

She dropped the rolling pin into the sink with a hollow thump and picked up the wooden handled butcher knife, wiping the edge clean with a dishtowel.

"I'll roll," Anna said, picking up the dough from the chair and laying it on the table. She folded it to pick it up, and then spread it out in a circle. Her fingers worked it as if she was rolling up carpet, when she finished it looked like a fat white snake.

Nellie drew the blade through the dough with one hand, pulling the half-inch long strips apart with the other. Anna tossed the noodles in the growing pile, separating them and giving them enough space as not to stick together. They continued the two-woman assembly line until the table was heaping with homemade noodles.

Nellie wiped her hands on her red and white checked apron and picked up the dishtowel. She wrapped it around the handle of the huge pot boiling on the stove and clanked it down on the stovetop. The aroma of the dried dill floating in the roiling tangerine colored stock filled the air. A soup bone, its meat nearly cooked off and showing the white smooth socket, rolled and lifted in the boiling pot. "We can put the noodles in anytime now." She turned the heat down on the pot, letting it simmer and stood back as her mother dropped handfuls of noodles into the pot. Tonight, the boarders would have an excellent meal.

* * *

The cool days of spring ended and May brought heat and sunshine. Nellie hung clothes on the line in the backyard. The dripping water from a white towel draped over her arm felt cool and welcome. Every Saturday, since the beginning of April, this was her domain: the big back yard, and five or six baskets of clothes and bedding. She started taking in laundry to earn some money, and hoped she would soon hear from one of the many mines where she applied for secretarial positions. She pinched the corner of a bed sheet and plucked a clothespin from her mouth, fastening it to the rope line stretched across the yard.

She turned when Barbara yelled as she came running across the back yard.

"Can I go to the matinee? Tom Mix is playing."

She bent and looked into Barbara's eyes, taking the two clothespins from her mouth and asked, "Did you clean your room yet?"

"Yeah." Barbara didn't blink a gray eye as she lied.

"Can I check it?" Nellie said.

"Forget it. I'll ask Grammy for the money," she said, "She loves me."

The words cut through Nellie like a knife. Her daughter intentionally played her mother against her in all matters. She knew exactly what to say and what to do and Anna would usually take her granddaughter's side.

Barbara stared back at her and slowly and deliberately crinkled up her nose. She squinted her eyes with a growing anger, and a threatening look.

"No," Nellie said firmly.

"I'm going anyway."

"I think different. I think you need to start acting like a respectable eleven-year-old, and I think that time is now." She had run out of patience and ideas, and considered picking up a switch that lay near the laundry basket.

"What's the problem back there?" Anna yelled from the window.

"She won't let me go to the matinee, Grammy," Barbara whined, and her high voice begged for pity.

"She didn't clean her room, Mama. She knows the rules," Nellie said, straightening up and cupping her hands around her mouth to make her voice carry.

"I cleaned it for her. I was all caught up with everything," Anna yelled back, her voice echoing off the wooden back fence that peeked through the tall dead and brown hollyhocks from last year.

Nellie looked down at Barbara and said, "I thought you told me you cleaned your room?" She waited for an answer with her arms crossed and tilting slightly back on her heels, rocking.

"Well, I meant... I was going to before I went. You just didn't give me a chance to finish," Barbara said.

"Just go," Nellie said. She was tired of doing battle. Besides, her mother would side with Nellie and she did not want that today. What she really wanted was her own place.

Nellie finished hanging the rest of the laundry and walked around to the front of the house. She leaned tiredly against the door of her yellow Buick with her arms crossed. Down the street, a line of kids waited noisily to get into the theater. Her daughter's voice stood out from the crowd, as she bragged about the money her Grandmother gave her for the movies. The group of kids surrounded her, and Nellie watched as her daughter basked in the limelight. She loved being the center of attention.

The warm sun dried the front of Nellie's wet dress, the black and white checks fading from the numerous washings. A button was missing in the front and gapped open just enough to show some white skin. She fished out a safety pin from the big front pocket and opened it, pinning it from the inside, leaving a thin silver line of metal visible.

An old truck chugged up the street toward her. It passed her slowly, stopping near the curb in front of her car. A hand stuck out the window and signaled her to come. The smell of motor oil burned her nostrils as she walked through the white cloud of smoke blowing from the tailpipe. The driver stuck his head out the window.

"That yer Bueek?" he asked, a long thin stogie hanging from his lips. She looked at the mop of curly red hair hidden under the well-worn black felt hat. His red beard was unkempt and bare in spots.

"Yeah," she said. She turned and quickly scanned the side of her car, thinking he might have scratched it earlier when she was in the backyard.

"Shere is purdy," he said, rolling the stogie back and forth across his thin lips with his hidden tongue.

"Yer Nellie, ain't cha?" the man said, lifting up one red eyebrow in an arch. Before she could answer, he threw out another question.

"Betcha don't know who I am now, do ya?" he asked in slow mountain drawl that she recognized from the folks that lived in the foothills of the mountain between Summerlee and Oak Hill.

"No, I can't seem to place you," she said. She frowned in thought. Her blue eyes studied his thin arms heavy with freckles on skin the color of a ripe peach.

The smile plastered on his face showed his enjoyment of the guessing game. She noticed his yellowed, stogie stained teeth, with the front one broken halfway off and worn smooth. The stogie moved up and down with each word he spoke, sticking through the gap left by the broken tooth. She expected the cigar to fall at any moment.

"Cornpone," he said, the still wedged stogie moving twice with the broken syllables.

The name meant nothing and she looked at him blankly thinking of corn bread. After all, cornpone is what everyone called it around here. She wondered if he might be selling it door to door.

"Come on now, I wuz in school with ya up until I quit in the seventh grade. That book learnin just wasn't for me. I prefurred to git to work and I did purty good fer myself as ya can see," Cornpone said. A look of pride beamed from his face as he patted the outer dented door of the smoking truck.

He shut the engine off and the explosive backfire made Nellie jump.

"Cornpone Miller," she said, "now I remember."

He reached out and opened the truck door with the outside handle. The inside handle had long since broken off, leaving a stub of sharpened metal. He jumped down from the seat that dipped permanently, imprinted with the weight of someone's bottom. The only form of cushioning was a rough-cut piece of deerskin. A spring stuck through it and parted the brown hairs, some of them sticking to the sharp point of the curled metal.

"Mind if I take a peek at yer mobile?" Cornpone said, reaching up and pulling the stogie out of his mouth.

"Fine with me," she replied, watching him carefully as he slid the unlit cigar down inside the top of his black scuffed up boots that nearly reached his knees. He was scrawny and tall, his white tee shirt smeared with burnt wood ash, and he smelled of wood smoke. His tee shirt appeared stuffed in the front of his jeans and the tail of it hung out the back, covering the worn bottoms of the pants. The pant legs, from just below the knees, were tucked and hidden inside the big boots.

He walked around the car, running his finger over the yellow paint. He squatted down on his knees and ran the palm of his hand over the thick rubber of the tires. He seemed to be talking to the tire when he said, "Real nice Bueek."

She remembered him from the seventh grade. Back then he lived with a moonshine-making Daddy in the foothills of the mountain.

The one thing that stuck in her mind was the time he came to school with welts as wide as a razor strop showing through the back of his tee shirt. She remembered him sitting at the desk in front of her and watching the little stripes of blood ooze through the material, and the teacher taking him back to the cloakroom to clean him up.

"So, I heard ya lived up in Charleston." He thrust up from his knees and stood. "Ya back to stay?"

"I don't know for how long, but there really wasn't any work left," Nellie said.

"Yep, the only thing keepin people round hear from starvin are the mines and I hear they might strike agin. Ya know Charleston purdy good, don't ya?"

"Uh huh, I've been all over it," she said.

"Ya workin?" he asked.

"Just helping my mother with the boarding house and taking in laundry. I get by, well enough, I guess," Nellie said.

"I know how ya could make some real good money. That is if yer intrested?" Cornpone looked at the ground and scuffed up the dust with the toe of his boot.

"Just how would that be?" she asked him. Her eyebrows arched high with suspicion.

"Well," he hesitated, "Meet me tonight down at Ruby's Diner, and I'll fill ya in. Round about eight wud be real good."

It wouldn't do any harm in meeting him she thought. Besides, if it were illegal, which she thought it was, she wouldn't have to go through with it. He opened the truck door and pulled himself up and onto the seat. The door slammed hollow and he looked straight ahead. The truck moved slowly away, hidden by a cloudy white smokescreen of burning oil.

* * *

Nellie sat in the parlor anxiously watching the hands of the clock. Barbara was sprawled on her stomach beside Anna, who watched the eleven-year-old coloring in a Tom Mix coloring book. She had won it as a door prize at the theater. Each Saturday they held a drawing and handed out prizes to the kids with the winning ticket stub. Barbara had switched her losing ticket with a little girl who did not understand the drawing.

The hands of the clock neared eight and Nellie stood up from the settee.

"Mother, I nearly forgot, I have to drop off the laundry over to the Hickam's house. I should be back in about twenty minutes. Could you watch Barbara?" she asked.

"Yes dear, I don't mind. She's good company when Frankie works nights," Anna said.

"I wanna go," Barbara said. She paused her coloring and looked at Nellie.

Nellie was waiting for an argument to brew when her mother said, "No, Grammy needs company."

"All right then," Barbara said. She pretended to be disappointed.

She left the house with the basket of ironed clothes and drove straight for Ruby's Diner just on the fringe of town. She pulled into the dirt parking lot and parked beside the rusted truck. The place looked vacant through the glass window extending the length of the rectangular shaped building. She shut off the engine and walked up to the screen door. Above it, a dim light attracted buzzing moths and June bugs flying blindly into it, and their clicking shells seemed to sound like tiny castanets.

Cornpone sat in a booth at the back of the diner recognizable by his black felt hat perched on his head like a miniature volcano. Nellie slid into the booth separated from him by a scarred table top, perched on a pedestal. Cornpone called to the waitress. She turned from behind the front counter as he lifted up his empty cup saying nothing. She returned with the pot and a cup for Nellie.

"Anything to eat?" she asked, filling Cornpone's thick mug and then Nellie's.

"No, thank you," Nellie said, picking up the sugar dispenser and pouring some into her cup.

"Not surprising," the waitress said. "Business been real bad these days."

She had a melancholy sound and look. Her skin matched the color of Cornpone's hat and her frizzy hair stuck out. She walked away from the table slowly with slumping, sad shoulders.

"How's tricks?" Cornpone said. His head was down and he blew noisily into the steaming coffee.

"All right, I guess."

"Your mobile a good runner?" he asked, still looking at the coffee. The point of his black hat aimed at Nellie's face like the tip of a big bullet.

"I take care of it," she answered.

"Well, like I told ya befer, I know how ya kin make yerself twenty dollars a trip." He slowly lifted his head up until his green eyes met hers.

"Running your shine, I suppose?"

"Yep."

"How many trips?" she asked.

He wet the tip of his finger with spit and tried to multiply on the tabletop.

"Eighty dollars for four trips," she said quickly.

"Yeah, eighty dollars for four," Cornpone said questionably. He had trouble with multiplying once he got higher than the three tables. He took her word for it.

"How much shine?" she asked. She had read the papers and knew possessing such a large quantity meant a bigger sentence.

"Hundert jugs each trip."

"That's a lot of weight. I don't think my car could carry that much at one time," she said. She knew it would be close to nine hundred pounds, and twenty years.

"I kin fix that. Bring your mobile up to the house tomorrow," he said. His tongue stuck out the gap left by the missing tooth and he flicked it.

"Can I think about it?" she asked. That was more money in a week than she made working in Charleston.

"Yep...for about another two minutes. I got another fellar intrested."

She could rent a place, she thought, and buy some furniture. She'd only have to do it until one of the mines called her for work.

"I'll go on the first run with ya," he said. "Show ya who, and where it goes to."

"When would that be?" she asked.

"Morrow night. After I sturdy up them springs on yer Bueek. Don't ya worry none. The revenuers ain't never gonna stop a woman."

She thought about the money and the chance of moving her and her daughter out of the boardinghouse.

"Well, what's it gonna be?" Cornpone asked, drumming his dirty fingernails on the table.

"I'll try it. You go with me tomorrow, and if I don't mind it, I'm in," she said. She took a drink of her coffee and ran her finger around the lip of the cup.

"One thing though," she looked at him. Twenty years in state prison was a long time. She put on her business face, the same look she used with tough customers at the glass plant.

"What?"

"Make it twenty-five a trip," she said.

His drumming nails on the table stopped abruptly. She saw his Adam's apple rise in his throat and then fall. She knew she had him.

"Ya drive a hard bargain," he said. He stuck out his dirty hand and she looked at it, shook it, and slid her hand under the table, wiping it on her dress.

"I have to go," Nellie said getting up from the table.

"I got yer coffee," he said, standing up and reaching into his pocket.

"Thanks," she said. "See ya tomorrow."

SIXTEEN
MOONSHINE AND MARIGOLDS

Nellie tromped her foot on the accelerator and the eight cylinders of the Buick roared like a West Virginian panther. Cornpone stuck his head out from under the hood and slammed it down with a bang. He wiped the sweat from his forehead and adjusted his black pointed hat.

"Ought to 'bout do it," he said. He tossed the screwdriver into a pile of rusted tools by the side of his shack. Nellie shut the car off, stepping out of it dressed in a pair of tight blue jeans and a red and black checked flannel shirt, the cut off sleeves ragged on the edges. A leather belt cinched her thin waist and the belt buckle was a rhinestone-covered horseshoe for luck. When she looked at Cornpone, she hoped the buckle was enough to bless her with a safe trip.

"Load her up, boys," Cornpone ordered, and three men came from the woods each carrying a wooden box. Inside each of them nestled ten jugs of the best moonshine in a three-state region. The three men silently repeated the trips from the woods to the car until all ten boxes were safely in the back of the Buick

A faint crescent moon hung in the twilight sky, and it would soon be dark. Nellie watched as the three men and Cornpone lowered the boxes into the compartment that he rigged up earlier. When the last box was in, they put the back seat over the compartment and bolted it down on both sides. The rear of the Buick remained level with the shims in the leaf springs and the heavy coil springs, salvaged from a wrecked Packard, holding the weight up as if there was nothing hidden.

Nellie walked to the back of the car and checked the back seat to see if anything looked out of place. Lowering herself to her knees, she looked under the car. The fake panels, riveted and puttied, wore yellow that matched the Buick. She nodded her head in satisfaction.

"Let's go," Cornpone said. "You boys watch the still and keep the smoke down." The three of them nodded in compliance. They walked single file down to the woods and disappeared on one of three paths. They melted into the forest without a sound.

Cornpone took a thin stogie from inside his boot, looked it over, and stuck it in his mouth. He jumped into the passenger side, slamming the heavy door. Nellie slid behind the wheel and pushed the clutch in, pressing the starter button. The Buick roared to life and the car lumbered slowly up the deeply rutted dirt road.

The thick steering wheel felt solid in Nellie's hands and she released her tight grip to cool her sweating palms. She pressed on the accelerator, testing to see if the Buick had enough power with the added weight. The automobile lurched forward and Cornpone's hat slid back on his head.

"Watch it," he said, reaching up and adjusting his hat.

She smiled, turning onto the back road that would bring her out onto the Oak Hill side of the Gauley Bridge. The headlights of the automobile held steady on the black road, proving that the extra weight was giving them a very solid and stable ride.

"Why do they call you Cornpone?" she asked.

"Long story," he said, the stogie sticking out of his lips, "Too long."

"I got plenty of time. It's two hours to Charleston."

"Well, if ya really want to know, I guess I kin tell ya," he said. His words poured out slow, settling in the car like thick syrup.

He nestled back in the seat and pulled the felt hat down over his eyes. The tattered brim rested on the bridge of his nose and he tilted his head back. His long legs stretched under the dashboard, and he cleared his throat.

"Well, we wuz real poor. My mama passed away the year I started second grade and my daddy could not cook for shit. I taught myself how to make corn pone. It was mostly all we ever had in the cabin anyhow." He moved around in the big bench seat and stuck his elbow out the window, resting it on the sill.

"Anyways," he continued, "I would up and take corn pone in my bucket every day fer my school lunch. The others thought it was queer, uh guess, and purdy soon they jist up and started calling me Cornpone. The name stuck to me like wild honey to a bear's tongue, so I jist left it that a way."

"What's your given name?" she asked.

"Same as my Daddy's was," he said, snorting with disgust.

"And that was?" she asked him. She seemed to have to drag each sentence out of his mouth.

"Moses. Just like the man who climbed that mountain in the Bible." Cornpone's head was still back and the hat slid lower on his eyebrows.

"That's a nice name. An honorable one, too," she said

"Where's your Daddy now?" she asked.

"Dead," he said.

"What happened to him?" she asked. "The mines?"

"Shit no. He done pizened himself on shine he bought offa some old gypsy man. It had enough rubbin alcohol in it to keep yer Buick running fer three cold winters. I found him down in the back yard, stiff as a board, his skin the color of a fox grape after the first frost."

"I'm sorry," she said.

"I'm not, he wuz worthless. When I found him, I felt like gittin his razor strop outta the house and whipping his dead ass. I let him lay out there till I couldn't stand the stink no more. Finally, his drunken uncle came by with two of his sons. I jist hid in the woods and watched them wrap his swelled old body in a hunk of tarp and drag him off. I don't even know where they buried him, and I don't care none. Fer as I'm concerned, he's providin heat down in hell with his shine soaked guts."

Nellie swallowed hard and stared straight ahead. She had never heard anyone talk that way about someone, especially their own kin.

"Who did you live with after that?" she asked.

He laughed quietly and scoffed. "Why'd ya think I quit in the seventh? I raised myself after that. I done been on my own since then and that's jist the way it's gonna stay," he said. He angrily pulled the hat down further, and in minutes, she heard him snoring.

Cornpone slept until the Buick was almost to the boulevard. Nellie turned right and drove eastward on Piedmont Road. She followed the New York Central tracks and made a left, driving south on Morris. Cornpone lifted his hat and rubbed his sleepy eyes. He squinted out the window.

"Where's the first stop?" she asked.

"Only gonna be one. The man wants all hundert," he said. "Broad Street by the depot. He has a black panel truck."

"Good. That's only three blocks away," she said. She turned onto Broad and drove north until she saw the train depot. A few automobiles were in the big gravel covered lot, but no sign of a truck.

"Round back," he said, "Clear round." He made a circle with his hand in the air.

She drove through the lot and ended up on the backside of the building. The black truck blended in with the dark. She pulled in behind it and shut off the car. Her stomach felt queasy, and she swallowed hard. Her blue eyes darted about, filled with fear.

"Wait here," he said. Cornpone stepped out and crunched across the gravel. A pudgy man in a dark suit and a gray hat leaned on the fender of the truck. Two other men stood at the back of the truck, one of them with his foot resting on the bumper.

Nellie strained to hear, but a passenger train approached and all she could see was their mouths moving. The man in the hat motioned for the two other men and they walked toward the Buick. One of them had a wrench in his hand. She sat stiff and still in the front seat.

The man with the wrench opened the door of the Buick and began to loosen the bolts. He did the same around her side of the car and they lifted out the seat. Removing one of the boxes, he pried the lid off with a screech of metal on wood. She stared ahead.

They walked back to the suited man, the man with the wrench also carrying a glass jug. He handed it to Cornpone and he unscrewed the lid of the jug off, presenting it to the man in the hat. The man sniffed it, and then tilted the jug, holding it with his fat finger through the glass handle. He brought the jug down to his side and she could see him smiling and shaking his head. The two men returned to the Buick and unloaded the cases, transferring them to the fat man's truck. They put the seat back tightly after the last load. The man in the hat pulled out a wad of cash and she watched as he peeled the bills off and laid them in Cornpone's outstretched hand.

They didn't say a word until they were safely out of the city, the Buick making excellent time now that it was empty. Cornpone turned to her and said, "Weren't so bad now was it?"

"No," she said. A bead of sweat slid down the center of her back.

Nellie drove on, watching him from the corner of her eye. His hand slid deep in his pocket and he pulled out the bills. He fanned through them and held them up to his nose, inhaling deeply. He started to laugh, quietly at first and then louder. He threw back his head and his roaring laugh vibrated through the back of her seat, tickling her spine.

It neared one-thirty in the morning when Nellie pulled up in front of the boarding house. In the low light, she fumbled with the key, trying to hit the lock. Finally, it slipped in, and she tiptoed across the dining room and up the stairs. She hid the money deep in a sock in her dresser.

The next morning Nellie watched sleepily as Barbara boarded the school bus. She went back into the house and poured a cup of black coffee. Anna pushed open the cellar carrying an armload of dirty mining clothes that belonged to the two new boarders. She tossed the clothes out into the laundry room.

"How was your trip? I heard you coming in late," she said. She poured a cup of coffee and sat down in a chair at the wooden table.

"Good. I had trouble finding a few of the offices, but all in all it was pretty uneventful."

Nellie slid out one of the wooden chairs and sat down across from her mother.

Yesterday afternoon, Nellie told her mother that a job offer came through for her, as a courier for three mines. She would be running weigh bills, memos, and the like to the main offices in Charleston. Anna was happy that she found a job in these hard times and didn't question her.

"I'll help you with the laundry," Nellie offered. She drank the coffee down and poured another cup.

"Great. I can start supper. It would be a big help," she said. Anna sipped from her cup. An annoyed look appeared on her face.

Nellie felt a lump growing in her tight throat.

"What?" she asked. She took a breath of air and held it.

"It's hard to get good coffee nowadays. It seems everybody wants to put chicory in it. That stuff makes it so darn bitter that you can hardly drink it."

Nellie exhaled. She replied with a sigh, "Well, I hope Roosevelt gets things straightened out soon."

Anna worked in the kitchen while Nellie scrubbed the boarder's coal crusted mining clothes. Nellie hung the clothes in the back yard on the line and walked to the front of the house. A horn blew from the street.

Cornpone was sitting in his truck waiting for her. She glanced around then ran up to the truck.

"Tonight, seven o' clock," he drawled with a low voice, his black hat covered with bits of straw.

"I'll be there," she said, nervously looking back toward the house. "You'd better go."

He released the clutch and the truck backfired as it rattled down the street. She walked to the back yard and finished hanging up the clothes. She kicked off her shoes and walked through the sole-tickling, soft grass.

Along the wooden fence, she admired the flowerbeds of azaleas, phlox, hollyhocks, and a variety of mixed wildflowers. She bent, looking close at a row of yellow and rust colored marigolds. She picked a few of them and held them to her nose. The peppery scent filled her head. She picked a few more and took them into the house, filling a vase with water and placing it in the center of the dining room table. The bright colors contrasted to the dark wood of the table. She called her mother into the room.

"Look. Mama," she said. "They add a nice touch, don't you think?"

"They sure do, dear," Anna said, reaching her hand out and stroking the small petals.

"I have to work tonight," Nellie said, "Could you watch Barbara?"

"Yes dear, I don't mind at all," Anna said. "How do you like it so far?" she added.

"It'll do until something better comes along," she said.

After helping her mother with supper, she drove out to the shack that Cornpone lived in. She took the winding road out of Oak Hill. She drove through patches of sun and into shade, where the hemlocks grew thick as a green walled fortress. She breathed in the heavy scent of pine. Lost in the beauty, she nearly missed the turnoff to the dirt road. She braked quickly and cut the wheels down the rutted and narrow dirt lane. Dust billowed behind the Buick as it bounced in the direction of the shack.

She pulled the car into the yard, unable to distinguish grass from the weeds. An old tractor body, orange with rust, leaned over as if it would fall. The wheel missing from one side, and the other embedded in the dirt, prevented that. She walked toward the shack.

To the right of the square leaning building, a conical pile of tin cans showed years of quick meals. Some glittered new, some already rusted, and some just getting there. Each one had their lids flipped open and edges rough from a hunting knife blade. The two-room shack, constructed with rough-cut lumber siding, tilted slightly to the front. The rusted stovepipe, serving as a chimney with its seams sealed with something the color of tar, leaned crooked.

At the door of the shack, she yelled through a rusted screen door ripped near the top.

"Anybody home?"

One dirty window with a broken pane cast a weak light inside and the place appeared deserted. She picked her way with high steps through the knee-high weeds in the back of the shack. There was an outhouse and more metal piled in rusted heaps; everything from bedrails to old automobile rims. She stopped suddenly, remembering Cornpone's dead father. Maybe this was the spot, she thought. She dashed toward the wood line.

Three paths led into the thick woods. She paused, studying them and trying to remember which one the men came out of yesterday. She chose the middle one. Bending, she lifted the thin branches of a spicebush out of her way and walked while crouched down through the tangles of greenbrier. She fought off the grabbing thorns that were clawing at her pant legs and shirtsleeves.

Thin limbs of a beech blocked her path and she moved it. Another thin one whistled through the air, whipping her right cheek with a sharp crack. She gasped and winced. "Damn," she hissed rubbing her cheek and feeling the skin rising immediately with a growing red welt.

She wiped the blood on the sleeve of her shirt and continued down the thin trail. Glossy leaves of mountain laurel lined the barely visible path. Cupping a hand to her ear, all she heard was the shrill cry of a startled chipmunk. It scurried away, rattling the bone-dry leaves. Clamoring downward, she found herself leaning back to control her balance and speed of descent. She thought she heard them, and stopped again.

The rustling of the mountain laurels to her right startled her and she quickly turned. A rough hand clamped over her mouth and she felt the pistol's cold muzzle chilling her neck. Her heart pounded and she stood frozen with fear. She felt a knee driving into the back of her leg herding her like a cow down over the hill.

They did not stop until they reached the bottom of a rock face. The man roughly pushed her up a snaking path littered with broken pieces of brown sandstone and she nearly tripped on a football-sized piece. A small cloud of smoke drifted out of the mouth of an overhang. A sharp stinging blow sent her nearly sprawling to level ground.

Cornpone was with two of the men she recognized from yesterday. One man fed wood to a fire under a big copper boiler while a coiled piece of copper pipe dripped a clear liquid into a glass jug. Cornpone squatted with his back toward her, holding up a jug and checking for clarity.

Smoke blackened the ceiling of the overhang that protected the boiler. The man behind her pushed down on her shoulder forcing her sit on the hard ground. Cornpone turned with a look of surprise and motioned with a nod of his head for the new man to move away from her. Cornpone's knees cracked with a pop when he stood.

"What the hell ya doing?" Cornpone said. His angry red face twisted. "Damn good way to git a bullet in ya." He turned to the man and pointed. "Marlow is muh brand new guard."

She looked at him, her eyes wide with fear, and said, "I didn't know. I went to the house. Since I couldn't find anybody, I decided to come looking for you." She rubbed the back of her neck, the muscles sore from the man twisting her head so roughly.

"Anybody see ya?" he asked.

"No, no. I didn't see anyone," she answered franticly.

"Ya better hope not," he said. His green eyes hid behind slits that scared her more than Marlow did.

Cornpone told the three men to get the cases ready and to bring them up to the shack. He looked at Nellie and said, "Let's get going. We're running behind as it is."

She got up from the ground, wiping dust from her jeans. They left taking a different route back to the shack. They drove to Charleston with their cargo and he barely spoke. It was the last trip he made with her. Her other promotions gave her a sense of accomplishment, but this one left her dry-mouthed with a queasy feeling that rolled in the pit of her stomach.

In two weeks, she had saved enough to rent a small house near the school: A five-room company house, painted gray, with a porch in the front. Nellie's mother watched Barbara for her while she did her illegal runs. One day, she received a call from one of the mines for an interview as a purchasing agent. After less than a month, she was able to make her last, and final, run for Cornpone.

Nellie dropped Barbara off at her mother's house, drove down Main Street past the theater, and turned left in the direction of Cornpone's shack. She was rounding a bend in the road when she noticed three cars setting on the side of the road by the lane that went down to the shack. The spinning red light on the sheriff's car threw red across the chest of a deputy leaning on the car. Two unmarked black cars with government license plates were empty.

She tried to look straight ahead on the road, but her frightened eyes drew to the man in uniform. Her knuckles gripped the steering wheel hard and the tightening knot in her stomach made her nauseous. The deputy nodded his head at her and she forced a weak smile. He waved her past. She watched the cars disappear in her rearview mirror.

She missed the knob twice trying to roll the window down. The third time, the cool air of October poured into the car. It was then that she saw him. He ran out of the wood's edge without his hat, his red hair drenched with perspiration. Waving his arms wildly, he ran while looking back over his shoulder. She slammed on the brakes and the Buick slid on the dirt road. He stumbled to the car and tore open the back door, diving onto the back seat. She tromped hard on the gas pedal and the Buick spun gravel and rocketed forward. The back door slammed shut with the forward momentum.

He stretched out flat in the back seat. Between loud coughs and wheezing, he said hoarsely, "Get me the hell out of here." She drove fast with wide nervous eyes checking the mirror. A rolling dust cloud followed her. The car bounced down every evasive back road she could think of, finally ending up in front of her house. She got out and Cornpone slithered from the back seat, his shirt ripped and mud stuck to the knees of his pants. The sole of his right boot gaped open and flapped like a mouth.

They ran into the house and she rushed from room to room yanking down plastic window blinds with loud zips. Cornpone slumped into the wing-backed chair close to the front door of the living room. Returning from the kitchen with a glass of cold water, she stood in front of him.

"Here," she said, thrusting out the glass with a shaking hand, "What happened?"

He guzzled the water, stopping only to take a forceful breath, and then drained the glass, handing it back to her.

"Revenuers," he said. His heaving chest rose and fell like bellows.

His open mouth gasped for air, and he held up a finger for her to let him catch his breath. Taking a huge gulp of air, he continued.

"They got the others, but I was back in the woods behind the cave, relievin myself. I heard the commotion and I seen 'em take Joe and Lamar up through the woods in shackles. I think they done shot Marlow. He wouldn't put the Colt down." He rubbed his face with his grimy hands. "But I don't think they saw me," he said through his hands.

"If they did see you, they'll be looking for you," Nellie said, taking the glass and walking back to the kitchen. She filled it up again. He drank it slowly this time.

"I gotta git out of here," he said. "I could go over to my cousin's place in Logan County." He wiped the dripping water from his chin with his shirtsleeve.

"Well, I think it's a good idea if you lay low until things calm down," she said, adding, "Got any money?"

"Naw, it's back at the cabin. The four hundert will not be there long though, I can tell you that much. Them revenuers will take it all," he said. "Damn them."

"I can get you on the bus," she offered. "It'll be leaving in about fifteen minutes."

"I'd be a might obliged to ya," he said.

She lifted the corner of the green window blind on the front door and peeked outside.

It was quiet except for the autumn wind blowing the leaves across the yard. She went to her bedroom, took fifteen dollars out of her dresser, and found a sweater that was much too big for her. She returned and tossed the gray wool sweater at him.

"Put that on. It will hide that ripped shirt." She pointed to the bathroom. "Wash the sweat off your face."

He did as she told him and, in few minutes, returned, his face wet. The sweater hung off him. She handed him the money and he jammed it into his back pocket.

"Let's go," she said, checking the alley in front of her house one more time from behind the front door blind.

She dropped him off at the bus station just in time for him to get his ticket to board the bus for Logan. He climbed the steps of the bus, his sole flapping on the boot. She watched until the red taillights of the bus disappeared into the night.

The next day she drove to Charleston and traded the Buick off to another shine runner, an acquaintance of the pudgy man. She traded him for a 1929 blue Graham Paige with a white soft top. She left Charleston in the car feeling a bit safer.

She never saw Cornpone again. Years later, she heard he found employment in the mines, but ended up taking a bullet through the forehead in one of the coal company strikes. It might have been a Pinkerton guard with an itchy trigger finger who got him. Someone else said Cornpone had shortchanged too many miners with watered down shine. However it happened, she figured the confusion of the riots allowed someone to draw a bead on him.

SEVENTEEN
FORGET ME NOTS

In the kitchen, Nellie's tired eyes roamed over the Sunday paper. Pausing briefly as she read the weather forecast, she shook her head. It was only the seventh day of December and already she had enough of the snow. Folding the paper, she looked out the window above the sink. Fluffy white flakes floated down adding to the snow already cresting on the branches and laying in the crooks of the trees.

She turned away, diverted to the sound of swishing curtains separating her daughter's room from her. Barbara walked slow and sleepy eyed into the room. It was almost noon. Nearly eighteen, Barbara had grown into very attractive teenager. Her blonde hair curled on the ends where it now touched her shoulders. She wore a white long-sleeved man's shirt, the tail sticking out, and blue jeans rolled high in cuffs above her calves. Black and white saddle shoes, with one white and one pink bobby sock turned down, showed the white skin of her ankles.

She ignored Nellie and went directly to the refrigerator. Bending at the waist, her head disappeared inside, and then she stood up, slamming the door shut. The force made a loud thud and caused the bear shaped glass cookie jar on top of it to rattle.

"Never is anything good around here to eat," she said. "Guess I'll go over to Katie's house." She grabbed an ankle-length wool coat hanging on a hook by the kitchen door and walked out the back door, slamming it as she left.

Nellie smiled, ignoring the outburst. She had found ignoring her actions sometimes to be the best form of discipline. It worked better than anything else she tried. Barbara hated not being the center of attention. The years of groundings, spankings, and taking her allowance did nothing in the way of changing the girl. The tantrums now were short and sparse. Barbara lived for attention and when it was not there she wore the face of defeat.

The ringing telephone interrupted the welcome quiet in the small house. Nellie slid the paper across the table, and walked to the living room.

It was Anna, chattering loudly and excitedly, telling her to turn her radio on. She set the phone down and walked quickly across the small room, nearly tripping on a piece of ripped linoleum sticking up in the air. She turned on the old floor model and it hummed as the tubes warmed. She returned to the phone.

"I'm back," she said. Before Anna replied, the announcer's voice drifted across the room. She leaned forward, her mother's breath in one ear, and the announcer's rapid-fire delivery in the other. The Japanese had bombed some place called Pearl Harbor. He painted a picture of planes swooping like mad bees. She said a quick goodbye and hung up. War had come to Oak Hill once again. She sat back in the chair and closed her eyes, listening to the report and remembering the pain brought by the last war. That terrible war: the one they had proudly proclaimed as "The War to End All Wars."

* * *

Nellie drove the long cream-colored Packard convertible up to the gas pump. She handed the ration card to the attendant and watched him study it. When he was satisfied that the card wasn't bogus, he unhooked the hose and pumped in the weekly three gallons of gasoline. Nellie thanked him and drove off. She glanced at the gas gauge, and tapped it with a long fingernail. The needle flicked and she hoped the quarter tank would get her to the airport and back.

She was picking up a client at the request of her boss. It was her ninth year as purchasing agent for U.S. Coal, and the company president was impressed with her shrewdness when it came to lowering the costs of materials. She had a knack for getting hard to find items since the war. He never asked how she did it, but it kept them in business and the output of coal couldn't be better.

The Packard rolled along the highway, its thick tires humming on the newly paved road. Through the big side window, she saw the redbud trees in full bloom. They dotted the sides of the mountains with a brilliant soft pink that matched her skirt and jacket.

Nellie found a spot, between an Army Jeep and a troop bus, and parked. Her heels clicked as she walked briskly to the terminal. Men in military uniforms rushed about the place. They wore their duffel bags slung over their shoulders, and a line of them waited at the far end of the terminal for the military planes that would take them to places like New Guinea, the Solomon's, and Europe. Seeing them brought back memories of Cotton and she knew that, for many, it would be the last time they would see their families.

She walked down a corridor where small private planes arrived. The man she was picking up was a pilot who worked for a steel company and volunteered to fly Corsairs from a factory in Connecticut as needed. He was the steel company's main purchasing agent and had ordered tons of coal from the mine. She wondered if he would look anything like he sounded on the phone. His voice was warm and smooth and there were times she hated to end their conversations.

A plate glass window afforded her a wide view to watch the busy action. A ground crew pumped fuel into one of the planes, and a fuel truck sped off, stopping quickly to fill another. Nellie glanced down at her watch. He should be arriving anytime, she thought.

Her reflection bounced off the glass like a mirror, and she brushed her blond hair off her forehead. Her eyes sparkled and her make-up was flawless. She took a small bottle of perfume from her clutch-purse, spraying a tiny amount behind her ears. Through her reflection in the window, she saw an airplane bank over the top of the mountain. Her eyes focused on her transparent self in the glass as she smoothed her skirt, and the small plane appeared to circle her heart. It made a wide turn and drifted toward the runway. Puffs of smoke rose from the chirping tires when they touched the concrete. The plane taxied over to the terminal and the canopy slid back. A handsome man stepped out onto the wing and jumped onto the ground.

A duffle bag in his hand swung with his confident swagger. The prop wash from a plane lifted his short dark hair, and he quickly held on to the aviator glasses hiding his eyes. His bomber jacket covered a muscular build, and his thin mustache turned up when he smiled at her through the glass.

The door opened and he stepped inside, walking toward her with an outstretched hand. "You must be Mrs. Bell," he said. "Pleased to meet you in person, now I can place a face to that voice I've heard for so long. I'm Johnny Roberts."

His strong grip felt warm on her hand and there was softness to his skin she did not expect to feel.

"It's Miss Bell," she corrected him. A quick glance of her blue eyes checked for a wedding band on his hand.

"The car is on the other side of the terminal," she said, motioning with her hand in the direction.

They walked out of the terminal and, within minutes, were heading back toward Oak Hill.

"How's everything going with the mines?" He asked her.

"Better than we expected. In fact, we are having trouble keeping up with the orders," Nellie said. She stole a quick glance at him.

"The steel mills are the same. The war has us behind schedule on nearly every order. We just don't have enough men. Some of our plants are nearly all women: Doing a good job I might add." He leaned toward Nellie, his brown eyes checking the gas gauge. His thick eyebrows frowned with mental calculation.

"Is the gauge right?"

"Yes, I'm afraid so. I could only get the standard three gallons. You know, with the entire

Nation on rationing, I couldn't tell you the last time this car had a full tank," she said.

"I hope we can make it back," he said. She thought, stranded with him would not be such a terrible predicament.

"Are there any stations on the way?" he asked, adjusting his aviator glasses on his face.

"One, and it's about forty minutes away," Nellie said.

"It'll be a long walk in those shoes," he said, smiling. Her high heels gleamed.

"I'd go barefoot first," she said.

"I would too if I had to wear those." The car filled with their laughter.

Light rain speckled drops on the windshield and Nellie searched for the wipers on the unfamiliar dash. Johnny pointed to the buttons just below the radio. She reached to press the button at the same time he did and his hand brushed the top of hers. She quickly pulled her hand back.

"Sorry," he said. He turned on the wipers and looked right. She noticed his confident smile in the reflection of the window.

The filling station appeared as the car reached the top of the hill. The engine coughed as it coasted off the road toward the square building.

"Pull in," he said, waving his hand toward the single pump.

"But, I ..."

"Don't worry," he said. The Packard rolled up to the pump and the engine sputtered to a stop. "Not a moment too soon," he added.

A young boy in a straw hat opened the door of the small wooden store. He walked over to Nellie's window. She rolled the window down and leaned away from the drizzling rain.

"Three gallons?" the boy asked holding the straw hat to his head. He studied her for a moment.

"Wait, you were here once today already lady, you got your limit."

"Fill it up," Johnny said, leaning over close to Nellie and sliding his glasses just off the bridge of his nose. His eyebrows arched above his unflinching brown eyes.

"Cain't do that mister," the boy said. He grinned at what he thought was Johnny's joke.

Johnny reached into the lining of his bomber jacket, took out a small black leather case, and flipped it open, handing it to the boy. He looked at the identification and closed it handing it back to Johnny.

"Yes sir. No problem," he said. He stepped quickly behind the car, unscrewed the big silver cap and began pumping the gas. The big hollow tank echoed briefly with the pumping stream of fuel.

"How'd you do that?" Nellie asked.

"Official government business. I fly the planes that the Army needs down south. They take it from there. My company gives me the time off that I need to help the war effort and I am authorized as an agent of the government to see that they get delivered," he said.

"How long have you been flying?" she asked.

"Since the first war. I flew in France, and when I came home, I continued flying for the fun of it. I love the freedom. Have you ever been up?"

"Goodness no," she said. "I think I'd be scared to death."

"Wanna try it? I'm in town for a week and I have to take the Corsair down to Mobile next Sunday. We could do it tomorrow," he said. His contagious smile showed straight, white teeth.

"I don't know," she said hesitating. The metal clank of the gas lid closed on the car and the boy strolled up alongside.

"That comes to three dollars and thirty cents." He nodded his head toward the pump and thrust out a grease-covered palm.

Johnny reached in his pocket and counted out four dollars handing it to the boy. "Keep the change," he said.

"Gee thanks, mister." A broad gap-toothed smile of appreciation filled his face.

"I'll get you reimbursed for that," Nellie said. She eased the car out onto the road.

"A plane ride with me would be payment enough," Johnny said.

"Maybe, I'll take you up on that," Nellie said. "Where are you going to stay while you're in town?"

"I don't know, any suggestions?" he asked.

"My mother has a boarding house," she said. "It's right across from the train station."

"Sounds good," he said. "Real good."

"I'll take you there and you can decide"

"Great."

"Oh, and about that plane ride, well at least I'll know where to find you if I decide to go." She smiled at him.

* * *

When Nellie arrived at her mother's the next morning, Johnny and Anna were sitting on the front porch. Anna waved to her as she stepped out of the car. Nellie walked down the sidewalk and stood leaning against the white column. Her blonde hair touched the shoulders of the silver blouse she wore loosely tucked into her gray slacks.

"Hello Mother," she said, bending down and giving her a peck on the cheek. "Hi Johnny," she added.

"Would you like some coffee?" Anna asked.

"No, I'm fine," Nellie said.

"Are you ready to go flying Nellie?" Johnny asked, getting up from the chair and shoving his hands in the pocket of the leather jacket.

"Sure, let's go," Nellie said, a broad smile on her face. "I'll tell you, though, I'm really nervous."

Johnny laughed softly and said, "It's fun, you'll see."

"We'll fly over the house, so look for us," he said, smiling to Anna.

"I will. You kids have fun," Anna said. She watched the car drive off and went into the house.

In the kitchen, Anna planned the meal for the boarders. She needed to pick up a few things in town and jotted them down on a list. Patting her apron pockets, she reached inside and realized she put the money safely away in the cookie jar yesterday. Lifting the heavy jar from the top of the refrigerator, she set it on the table and removed the lid. It was empty. A few days earlier, it held eighty-four dollars.

At the airport, Johnny rented a two-seater Piper Cub. He helped Nellie up onto the wing and closed the small door. Walking around the plane, he made a quick pre-flight check. Twisting his way into the cramped quarters, he adjusted the seat. She watched him flip switches, check gauges, and key the microphone.

He slid on a headset and looked at her, smiling. She returned a weak, nervous smile.

"Calm down, you'll love it." He gave her a reassuring pat on the shoulder.

He radioed the small tower and taxied out onto one of the two runways. Nellie bit her bottom lip and clung to the door handle. He pulled the plane to the edge of the runway and waited for clearance. The engine revved with vibrating fingers that tickled her back through the small seat. Slowly the plane rolled and she covered her eyes.

She felt herself pushed back into the seat and her belly tickled when the rear wheel cleared the ground. Her shriek of excitement and fear filled the small cockpit. She reached over and grabbed onto his hand. He looked at her for a moment as the little plane continued its climb, and squeezed her small hand in his.

Johnny banked the plane southward, flying over patchworks of farmland, and buzzed in the direction of Oak Hill. Nellie's searching eyes found the bridge she traveled across so many times. They skimmed the mountaintops and watched another plane as it flew a thousand feet below them. She loved the feeling and the glow on his face that expressed his love for it. She understood what he meant now about loving the freedom it brought.

When they reached Oak Hill, they flew over the coal tipple and circled low over her mother's house three times before she finally came out. He tipped his wings at her and Nellie watched Anna waving from the yard below. He flew her over her own house, then back to the airport. Afterwards they had dinner at a restaurant in Charleston and he drove her car back to Oak Hill.

When he parked in front of the boarding house, they kissed without hesitation.

"I had a wonderful time. Could I see you again?" he said, brushing his fingers on her soft cheek.

"Yes," she said. She looked into his brown eyes and felt something she had never felt before. It was a feeling greater than her first love.

"Tomorrow?" he asked as he nuzzled his face into her neck.

"Tonight," she said.

He saw her every day until he left to take the plane to Mobile. She drove him to the airport and he surprised her with a bouquet of fresh picked Forget-Me-Nots. She watched him take off, staying until the plane flew completely out of sight. The drive back to Oak Hill had her feeling empty. How could I miss him already? she thought. Tears came, and she pulled off the road. She was in love and could not deny it.

Two weeks later, he returned, as promised, bringing welcome news. He applied for a transfer to a plant in Wheeling. Time passed and they became inseparable. He attended Barbara's high school graduation with her, and stood by her when Barbara ran off to Chicago with a man twice her age. While they waited for the transfer to come through, he continued delivering the much-needed planes.

Both of them equally hated being apart. They agreed the days were empty without each other's company. Johnny planned to change that soon.

* * *

The orange sun hung in the sky in June 1943, glowing with a brightness promising a spectacular sunset. He drove her to a place she had never seen in all her years in Oak Hill. The seldom-used winding road led to paradise. Parking the car at the road's end, he carried a blanket and a bottle of wine. She walked along with her hand on his shoulder. At the crest of the rise, he spread the blanket out and they sat in silence.

The sun touched the tops of the mountains. Katydids sang out from their hiding places in pines and low-growing huckleberry bushes. Honeysuckle scent floated in the twilight air. She saw a stand of beech trees with elephant skin bark. Dark initials scarred the thick trunks with promises of eternal love.

He opened the wine with a penknife and held it up to the sun, examining it. Satisfied, that little of the cork ended up in the dark red liquid, he offered it to her.

She tilted the bottle to her lips and sipped from it. The smooth, fruity taste quenched her dry throat.

"Thank you," she said. "It tastes pretty good after our little hike. It sure was worth it, though. This place is magnificent."

He took a drink and set the bottle down in a hole eroded in the slab of gray rock.

Scooting on his knees, he moved around to face her.

"I have some good news for you." He took her hand.

"What?" she whispered. She leaned close.

"They've approved my transfer," he said, smiling as he took her hand in his.

"That's wonderful!" she yelled, her voice echoed off the darkening thick stand of trees.

"I have something else too," he said. His deep voice carried to her with a rich, low tone.

She watched as he picked up the wine bottle and took a long drink. He offered her the bottle and she took it. It made her feel warm inside, and she unbuttoned the top collar of her yellow blouse.

Johnny stayed on his knees his back straight as he searched in the pocket of his pants. He pulled out a small box and looked at her.

"I have never felt for anyone as I feel for you, Nellie."

He swallowed hard and took her left hand in his. He opened the box and took out the ring. The solitary diamond glinted in the fading light.

"I want you to be my wife," he said, his finger poised to place the ring on hers.

"Oh, Johnny," she said, tears running down her cheeks. "Yes, I love you and I want to be with you the rest of my life." He slid the ring on her finger and they lay back on the blanket facing the peeking stars.

They made love that night in the darkness of the woods. When they left the overlook, he stopped at a barrel-sized beech, untouched, without a single blemish on its bark. With his penknife, and by the light of a burning pine branch she held high over him, he carved a heart the size of a dinner plate. Inside he added their initials, and underneath them, the word "Forever."

EIGHTEEN
LEGALITIES

Elaina carried bits of the gray January weather on her when she walked into Nellie's room. Her wet black hair and the shoulders of her tan coat were freckled with melting snowflakes. She handed Nellie the large yellow legal envelope and sat on the edge of the bed.

"That's everything you need Nellie." Elaina said.

Nellie slid her glasses on and opened the thick envelope. She scanned the documents, finding everything in order. The lawyer that was handling the hearing was the daughter of her old friend back in Oak Hill. Nellie discovered the lawyer's mother had retired and lived in Florida, and her daughter now headed the firm. Her lips moved silently when she saw the scheduled hearing date. It was on her seventy-fifth birthday.

Nellie's lip quivered and Elaina moved from the bed to take a seat on the arm of the chair saying, "It'll be all right, Miss Nellie, and don't you worry about a thing. Not a soul knows anything about this. Now cheer up, you're almost free."

"I'm still afraid," Nellie said. She put the documents back in the envelope with trembling fingers.

"Well, this might cheer you up. I got permission to take you out on a day pass. I told the director that I'm taking you out to eat." Elaina's mischievous smile grew. She patted Nellie's shoulder and continued.

"But what they don't know is the lawyers are going to meet you at my place."

"Outside? I haven't been out of this building since I got here; at least not off the grounds," Nellie said.

"Well, we're gonna have us some fun. I'll tell you that much." Elaina patted Nellie's hands and said, "Just you wait and see."

Nellie was grateful that someone as special as Elaina happened along and considered her very own guardian angel. The trusting of Elaina came easy after the years with Barbara. Nellie's knack for reading a person had always been sharp and she was sure, under normal circumstances, she would have never signed anything Barbara or her husband had shoved her way.

"Can you come back later?" Nellie asked.

"Sure, but right now I have to lock these up in my car," she said, glancing at the yellow envelope resting on the arm of the chair.

Elaina walked to the door carrying the envelope under her arm.

"Elaina?"

"Yes, Miss Nellie?" Elaina turned.

"Thank you so much," Nellie whispered quietly across the small room.

For the next few days, Nellie could barely contain her excitement. Sleep did not come easily, and when it did, it was restless. When Elaina walked into the room waving the pass in her hand, Nellie was dressed and ready.

"You look beautiful," Elaina said.

"Thank you," Nellie replied. She performed a weak curtsy and then spun around slowly in her flowered dress. Her gray hair was pulled back in a bun held by a comb, exposing dangly silver earrings glimmering in the weak light.

"Sure looks like you're ready. Let's go," Elaina said, "I have to have you back by seven." Nellie picked her coat up from the bed and slid it on.

When they walked by Banks' room, he raised his head off his pillow and tried to wolf whistle, but it was more air and spit than noise. For some reason, Nellie could not quite understand why she felt guilty for going outside when she saw Banks. Sure, he tormented her, but she suddenly felt like she had the time she saved a puppy from the animal shelter. She had shivered thinking about the sentence that lay in store for the puppies left behind and she now felt that way for Banks.

They walked out into the sunny January morning trailing puffs of silvery breath in the cold. Nellie held on to Elaina's arm and made their way across the parking lot to Elaina's fifteen-year-old car. Elaina opened the door and Nellie pulled herself onto the front seat. Elaina helped her with the seat belt.

The old car sputtered with contempt, and the starter ground with a screech. Just my luck we will not make it out of the parking lot, Nellie thought. The stubborn engine finally caught and the loud car rolled slowly onto the street. The noisy exhaust rumbled over Nellie's deeply exhaled sigh of relief.

Nellie twisted and turned in the seat, her eyes drinking in the sights. She pointed at homes, fast food joints, and supermarkets. She remarked about people they passed, and rolled down the window to smell the aroma of civilization. She breathed in a million fragrances blowing in through the open window: Roasted chestnuts from somewhere, popcorn from a vendor when they stopped at a red light, and the smell of cut flowers as the car idled near a florist shop.

Her ears tuned in to sounds she had long ago forgotten back in West Virginia. Dogs barking, children laughing, and the new voices of people filled her head. She felt alive again. It was just what she needed. The book of memories brought her back from death, and now this: The rejuvenation brought on by this taste of freedom was the transformation she needed.

"Play some music," Nellie said.

"Anything particular that you like?"

"Anything."

Elaina turned on the radio and crackling country music filled the car. Nellie followed the beat with her palm tapping on her knee. An older man pulled up beside them at a stoplight, and Nellie threw him a kiss. Elaina laughed as the old man stalled the car then lurched through the changing light.

Nearing the complex where Elaina lived, the view changed. Nellie frowned at the blowing newspapers, shards of broken bottles, and bits of discarded household furnishings. A mattress and a splintered headboard lay against a graffiti covered building. Its windows were replaced with plywood. Elaina turned into a paved lot, with cars setting on flattened tires, while others were on blocks that were left by tenants long since gone.

She parked the car in front of the complex and got out. A group of young men on the sidewalk stared as they watched Elaina open the door and help Nellie out of the car.

"You just better go on," Elaina said to them, her voice taking on an inner city command. They looked at her, their heads low and hidden behind hunched shoulders under jackets advertising membership in the neighborhood gang. They pranced like bristling hyenas in high top basketball shoes. Turning back to size up the quarry, the leader's eyes met Elaina, whose cold gaze of a protective lioness stared unflinching and hard. He turned, moving slow up the sidewalk, with the remaining pack following at his heels.

Once inside the small apartment, she helped Nellie off with her coat. She offered her a seat on the couch.

Elaina said, "Well, this is it." She silently showed off the organized and tidy living room, with a sweep of her arm. She took off her coat, picked up Nellie's from the couch, and hung them carefully to balance the tilted brass coat rack with a missing leg.

"How about some real coffee?" Elaina asked.

"Absolutely. You know I've waited for a cup of good strong coffee for a long time," Nellie said.

"Great, I'll be right back."

Elaina disappeared through an open doorway leading to the tiny kitchen. Nellie noticed the pictures on the wall of Elaina with a girl who Nellie guessed might be two years old. She bent closer, and noticed a striking resemblance between the two.

The sound of the electric coffeemaker gurgled and Nellie sniffed the aroma of brewing coffee. She leaned back into the softness of the couch.

Elaina walked back in the room with a cup in her hand.

"I cheated," she said, "I figured you were anxious so I poured it before the pot filled. It might be strong."

"Thank you so much," Nellie said. She drew the cup to her mouth with both hands and sipped it immediately.

"Good?" Elaina asked.

"Best coffee I have had in years," Nellie replied, taking another drink and setting the cup down on a coaster on the coffee table in front of her. Nellie looked up at the picture on the wall, comparing the little girl to Elaina who sat in a chair across from her.

"What?" Elaina asked, noticing Nellie's puzzled look.

"Whose little girl?" Nellie asked, pointing at the picture up on the wall.

"That's my pride and joy, Kareena," she said. "She'll be four in September. She is in pre-school now. After school, she goes to the sitter, and I pick her up around eight, unless, of course, I work nights. On that shift, I don't see much of her," she said disappointedly.

"Elaina, I never knew you were married. You never told me," Nellie said, picking up her cup poised to take a drink.

"I'm not, Miss Nellie," she said, looking down to the blue carpet of the living room floor.

"Oh, I see. Divorced?" she asked in a quiet voice.

"It's a long story."

"I got time, and nothing but. Unless, of course you don't want to get into it," Nellie said.

"Well, I've never really told anyone, but sometimes things just eat away at you and I guess if you don't let someone know, sooner or later whatever it is will just come and gobble you up, body and soul," Elaina said, a slight twang appearing in her soft voice. She rose from the chair, slid the picture from the wall, and sat down beside Nellie. She ran her thin finger across the front of the glass as if she was stroking her child's face.

"I came here years ago from a real little old town, just north of Valdosta, Georgia," she began.

"I know where that is. Mrs. Martz taught me," Nellie said. They giggled. Elaina continued in a soft, serious voice.

"Well anyway, my Mama married this man named Bricker. That was after my real Daddy passed on. Bricker had six kids of his own. Well, with my brothers and sisters, that made fourteen of us living in this old shotgun shack out in the middle of the Georgia clay."

Nellie noticed she seemed to be talking to the picture.

"It was real hard. He worked in a sawmill and my mama took in washing or whatever she could to feed us kids. It was more like a litter, if you know what I mean. Bricker was mean to Mama and my kin. He always was taking sides with his own. I wanted out in the worst way, Miss Nellie." She continued to look down at the picture.

"One night he drank so much he beat up my Mama real bad. It wasn't the first time either. She didn't love him. I never thought she did, but she needed whatever little cash he would bring home when he didn't spend it all down at the juke joint. "

Nellie watched Elaina's fingers gripping the picture and little bands of white appearing across her brown knuckles.

"So one day I screamed, enough was enough. My Mama was on the floor of the kitchen. He done knocked her out cold. He looked at me with enough hate for ten men, and I was scared. I ran out the front door as fast as I could and he caught me up behind the pigpen. She turned her head slowly and her painful brown eyes met Nellie's.

"He raped me that night, Miss Nellie."

Teardrops spilled over from her eyes, magnifying the picture of the girl in salty spots where they landed on the glass.

"It's all right, Elaina. It's all right," Nellie said.

Elaina wiped her forearm across her eyes and looked at Nellie. Her bottom lip quivered and she clenched her jaw, "I ain't never been back, and I never will. I could have got rid of my baby, but when I felt her move in me, I just could not do it. She brings me more happiness than anything else in this mean old world does. We don't have much, but we got each other and the day I packed up that old car out there," she pointed toward the window, "I knew I'd never go back there."

Nellie looked at Elaina and said, "You are not the only one in the world who has lived through that. You might find it hard to believe, but nearly the same thing happened to me. But Elaina, my wish for you is that your little girl turns out to be a better person than MY daughter did."

The two women spent time talking about their lives, and Elaina shared a scrapbook with Nellie that she had started when Kareena was born. They were looking through the scrapbook when a knock interrupted them. Elaina rose from the chair and looked through the door's peephole, spying two well-dressed women carrying briefcases.

"The lawyers are here, Miss Nellie," Elaina said, unlocking the door.

Nellie's heart pounded when the two women stepped inside and introduced themselves. Nellie stood, looking at Andrea Galloway, and remarked to her how much she resembled her mother, Bonnie Kay. Andrea told her she remembered her mother telling her stories about Nellie.

"Would you all like some coffee or anything?" Elaina asked, motioning them to have a seat. She hurriedly walked to the coffee table and picked up the scrapbook. The lawyer from Texas sat in the loveseat and placed her briefcase on the small glass coffee table, opening it with a click. Galloway asked Nellie to have a seat and join her on the couch.

"I'll be in my bedroom if anyone needs anything," Elaina said.

"No. I want you here," Nellie said.

Elaina looked at the lawyers who shrugged and smiled at her. She lowered herself to the floor and sat cross-legged near the coffee table.

"Oh, by the way, my mother sends her wishes," Galloway said.

"How is your mother?" Nellie asked politely.

"Oh, just fine. You know mother. Cantankerous as ever, and golfing every day." She set her briefcase across her lap, opening it with a snap.

"Well, let's get down to business," Galloway said, taking out a stack of papers and setting them on the table.

"These are your tickets to freedom; I took the liberty of getting twenty-eight signed affidavits from back in Oak Hill. They are all highly favorable to your case and are from people who have known you for many years. They contain strong evidence that you were and still are capable of living independently." She patted the stack of papers and smiled.

The other lawyer took out hospital records from the nursing home and from Oak Hill. She laid them out and said, "These only strengthen our case. You're healthier than I am," she laughed. Nellie felt relieved at the evidence, but looked at the lawyers, her eyebrows wrinkled in thought.

"What is it?" Galloway asked, noticing the look of puzzlement.

"Barbara. What about Barbara can't she...?"

Andrea interrupted her. "Nothing, Miss Bell, she can't do a thing. In her hurried attempt, she neglected to double check if she had the power of attorney. Hard to believe she is married to a lawyer, but I've seen stranger things in my twenty years of practice." She held up her finger and waved it back and forth in the air.

"We also have this."

Galloway reached into her briefcase and pulled out a packet of papers stapled together in the corner, they rustled through the quiet room as she leafed through pages.

"Miss Turner and I," she nodded toward the other attorney, "hired a private investigator and, through his investigation, proved this is not the first time your daughter has pulled something like this. She did the same to the mothers of her two previous husbands, with a little help from someone familiar." She flipped a page on the report and continued.

"She and her new husband, the lawyer, had an ongoing affair, you could say. The two of them worked together, filing the documents, selling the properties, and filling their own bank accounts. Your daughter would then file for divorce, using her lawyer friend, and end up with an equitable distribution of her marital assets. She lived quite well, and of course, the long-term plan was for their affair to lead to marriage, which it did. You were next on a long list, Nellie." Galloway said.

Nellie shook her head in disbelief.

"We have corresponded with both of them, and they've agreed to take what they have and run. They're concerned about some pretty lengthy prison time should any of these individuals decide to prosecute. Her previous husbands feel their compensation occurred the day she walked out of their lives. Unfortunately, the women they scammed were confined to other care facilities, and are no longer with us," she said, her voice trailing with sadness.

The other attorney spoke up saying, "But you could prosecute."

"I couldn't do that," Nellie said. "I don't want anything to do with her; that's a fact, but I don't want to see her in jail. She's over fifty years old. She can just live with what she has done."

"We figured you would feel that way," Miss Turner said, "But we just wanted to let you know your options."

Turner cleared her throat and said, "Now for the really good news." She looked at Galloway, expecting a cue. Galloway nodded her head for her to continue.

"There will be no hearing: I already met with Judge Hickam in Dallas. I understand that Elaina will be going with you back to West Virginia as your personal nurse. Is that correct?" she asked.

"Of course," Nellie said. She glanced at Elaina and smiled.

"Good, that was one thing the judge stipulated, that someone would be with you for care. So if you will just sign these documents, we'll be on our way."

Turner handed Nellie a pen, and placed the documents in front her, removing them one at a time as she signed them. She handed Elaina a copy of each.

"Congratulations, Miss Bell. I'll file these today, and as of midnight tomorrow night, you are a free woman," Galloway said, smiling.

Nellie looked at them, her mouth open and tears streaming down her face. Elaina screamed with joy, banging her heels on the carpet. They stood up, embraced, and the women walked to the door. Elaina sprang up, landed on her feet, and opened the door. After they exited and she closed the door, Elaina slumped and leaned her back against it. She looked at Nellie, her eyes red with tears.

She said, "You did it Miss Nellie, and you're free as a bluebird."

Elaina stepped slowly across the room and sat beside her. Nellie looked at her and took her hands in hers. She stroked the skin on top of her black hands and smiled, "No dear, we are BOTH free."

* * *

On the trip back to Beacon Manor, Nellie had Elaina make two stops. One at a McDonald's for a biggie-sized fish sandwich meal for Banks, and then at a K-mart, where she had the bag boy carry out to the car and put in the trunk five cases of Coke, six bags of ice, and a genuine child's slate chalkboard complete with the chalk.

Elaina managed to get the Coke past the newly hired night nurse, who felt shunned over the employee's party scheduled for next week. Why hadn't anyone told her until now, she wondered. She figured it would be okay to store the ice and Coke in the walk-in cooler of the kitchen.

That night several aides complained of an unusual amount of burping from every patient, and that they had refused their medication. One woman slapped a cup of lukewarm water out of an aide's hand and mumbled something about more soda pop.

In addition, the aides told the head nurse that the screeching of chalk from Martz's room might be the cause of the other patient's gastric reactions. When the nurse investigated and told the elderly former teacher that it was time to put her chalk away, she wrote in big wide letters on the board, "NO." Gordon Banks slept with a smile through it all. His lips wore a chocolate milkshake mustache, and an empty McDonald's bag lay crumpled at his feet.

NINETEEN
LOVE IN A MIST

Nellie and Johnny settled on a September wedding. In the parlor, an excited Anna pinned and re-pinned the hem of the bridal gown draping off Nellie. Anna rose with a groan and stepped back. Cocking her head, she mumbled something with the straight pins held by her lips. She knelt once again to change a part of the hem that did not meet her artistic eye of approval. Nellie impatiently fidgeted on the footstool she stood on.

"Keep still," Anna said.

Nellie looked down at the top of her mother's gray hair and shifted her foot.

"There you go again, I swear we'll never be ready in two weeks," Anna said, slowly rising until her eyes met the neckline of the gown. She smoothed down the ruffles around the neck and stood back, eyeing the gown from top to bottom.

"There, now go change and I'll get to work tomorrow on that hem."

"Thanks Mother, I really do appreciate all your help," Nellie said, stepping off the stool and nearly falling, Anna caught her by the elbow, and rolled her eyes.

"I swear if you lose one single pin out of that hem," Anna threatened to swat her behind.

Nellie laughed, bunching up the long gown in her fingers. She swished through the dining room and up the steps. Undressing, she placed the gown flat on the bed and changed into a pair of slacks and a sailor's blouse. She pulled her hair up quickly, and clipped it with a tortoise shell barrette. Through the window, she looked at the trees on the mountain. They were beginning to lose their dark green summer color. Before long, they would change into their fall brilliance. She ran her hand up the rough board that framed the window, her thoughts drifting to Johnny.

How lucky she was to have met him, and how he had made her life so much richer and fuller. He was perfect in every way, she thought. He would be coming tonight with another plane and they would be together. She could hardly wait. It had been nearly two weeks this time. She closed her eyes, imagining his face, happy and handsome, with his hair tousled and windblown.

Just a month ago, in Wheeling, they looked at a house for sale. The landscaped yard contained several manicured flowerbeds, one near the front with a flower Nellie knew as Love-in-a-Mist. They were stout plants and the purple petals contrasted among the white ones. He knew little about them and she explained they would not last. They were a one-season plant, an annual.

She remembered how he listened, and could almost hear his voice in the room, when he said, "They are not like us then, are they? Because, our love has bloomed into forever."

The chiming of the grandfather clock in the parlor prodded Nellie to glance at her watch. He would be at the airport in less than two hours.

Nellie arrived at the terminal and parked the new car: A reward she purchased with her recent raise. Inside, she stood in the familiar spot that afforded her a wide view of the mountain. She found the landmark he told her he used and set her sight on the tallest tree on the top. She checked her watch, noticing he was running late. But, it was not the first time. The weather often played havoc with his schedule when he would be forced to dodge thunderclouds or heavy turbulence. She decided to grab a bite to eat in the airport's small restaurant.

A waitress in a pink dress with a white scalloped bib walked over to her booth. She looked young to Nellie, nineteen or twenty, she guessed. She stood by the table with her order book perched in hand and chewed loud on a wad of gum. Between pops and snaps of the gum she asked, "What'll it be?"

"Do you have a menu?" Nellie asked.

"Up there," she said, chewing on the gum and pointing with her elbow.

Nellie looked past the girl's elbow and saw a menu written in chalk leaning up against the wall at the very end of the lunch counter. Nellie squinted to see and settled on a cup of soup.

She ate quickly, interrupting her meal with glances at her watch. Anxious, she left half of it, paid the waitress and went back to watch for the plane.

An hour passed and she paced, thinking something must have happened.

A man stood at the counter and she decided to check with him. Then she saw it: A small black dot to the right of the tree. It grew. It was Johnny's plane. She watched him circle wide and land. When he finally walked into the terminal, she held him tight.

They drove from the airport to Nellie's house. She showed him some dried flowers she made for the wedding. She even included some of the Love-in-a-Mist she picked when they looked at the house in Wheeling. They spent the night together, and in the morning, ate breakfast at Ruby's Diner outside of town. While they ate, they talked about the upcoming wedding.

"Did your daughter decide if she was going to be your bridesmaid?" he asked.

"She said she couldn't make it," Nellie said. She shrugged her shoulders and looked at him disappointed.

"I'm sorry," Johnny said. His comforting voice offered some consolation to her. She thought Barbara would at least have the decency to attend her wedding. It was all she talked about when she lived at home: How she wanted Nellie married, and how nice it would be to have a man around the house.

He fiddled with the napkin while they waited for a refill of coffee. Nellie sensed something was wrong. Johnny rarely showed nerves.

"Are you getting cold feet?" she said, smiling at him and reaching over and hooking his pinky with hers.

"No, no, it's not that at all," he said. "I just had a rough time with the plane last night and I'm wondering what could be the problem."

"I was worried too."

"I think it's a carb problem, nothing major. It's just running a little too rich. I'll take care of it tomorrow before takeoff. So I hate to say it, but I'll have to leave a little early."

The waitress returned with the coffee.

"Well, I'd rather see you safe, so if you have to be there sooner, it's not a problem with me. I'll be glad when the war is over and all of this traveling is behind us."

"That's why I love you so much," he said, puckering his lips and blowing a kiss across the table. She returned to him a teasing wink.

* * *

In the morning, they stopped for a quick visit with Anna and Frankie. Johnny laughed when Frankie told him the story of the ring in the pudding. Anna made him a lunch and packed it in an old dented miner's bucket she had in the cellar. He told them to take care of Nellie and that he would see them in two weeks for the wedding.

Nellie drove him to the airport and waited in the terminal, watching him as he worked under the cowl of the plane. He tested the engine a few times, looking up at her with a smudge of grease on his cheek. She watched him turning screws, and cocking his head to listen. He left the plane running, ran into the terminal, and kissed her. She held him until he reminded her he was behind schedule and had to have the Corsair in Mobile as soon as he could.

"I love you, Nellie," he mouthed through the glass of the canopy, then taxied onto the runway. She watched until the plane was out of sight.

* * *

The drive home seemed as long as it always had when he left. At home, she spent the rest of the night at her desk writing invitations for the wedding. She had wanted to send them out sooner, but it was mostly local people and the only real out-of-towners would be her Aunt Phyllis and Uncle Jim from Charleston. Johnny's only surviving relative was a sister in Ohio and Nellie sent her an invitation a week ago. She placed the last invitation in an envelope, licked it, and sealed it. She carefully set it on top of the others, and picked up the dried flowers. She touched them softly and laid them on the desk beside the invitations.

* * *

Johnny banked the plane eastward and decided to follow the Smokey Mountains. A heavy mist hung over the mountains and he climbed higher out of the clouds. The plane was flying perfectly and the controls seemed flawless. He trimmed the flaps to get more elevation and rose toward a break in the clouds that looked less than a mile away. He slowly pulled back on the stick and the plane floated effortlessly. He settled back relaxed, enjoying the view of a setting sun, and soon found that the night had surrounded him.

Thousands of feet below him, a long-bearded old hermit stood on the back porch of his cabin tucked away in the Smokey Mountains. Awakened by a full bladder, he stood on the porch of his shack, sleepily fumbling with the buttons on his pants. He paused, his attention drawn to the hum of an engine. Above him, the night sky hid twinkling stars peeking from behind the heavy white mist of low clouds. The engine grew louder, and his eyes searched the sky for the intruder daring to trespass on his accustomed silence.

A ball of bright orange caused the hermit to shield his eyes with a grubby hand. A deafening boom followed, rattling the shakes of his roof and vibrating the boards under his bare feet. The hermit shuddered as airborne flotsam sprinkled down to rustle the dark leaves. Suddenly, he remembered the childhood tale of the floating, glowing pumpkins that swallowed bad mountain children. He stumbled into his cabin and trembled under ragged covers.

* * *

Nellie knew there was a sense of secrecy to Johnny's job delivering the planes. There were times that flight plans changed in mid-air. He told her that; however, three days passed without any word from him. She looked at the phone and decided against using it, concentrating instead on the purchase orders in front of her.

The phone rang, startling her, and she breathed deep before answering it.

"Hello, Purchasing," she said, with her ear pressed hard to the receiver. The office downstairs required a purchase order number. She assigned them a number, logged it, and glanced at the clock. Seven more long hours of trying to concentrate remained.

Nellie decided to spend her lunch hour with Anna. In the kitchen, Anna concentrated on packing several miners' lunch buckets lined up on the sink.

"Hello, Mother," she said from the doorway of the kitchen.

Anna turned with a startled look. "I swear you're going to give me a heart attack one of these days," she said. She held her hand over her heart feigning an oncoming attack, but did not bring a smile to Nellie's serious face.

"What's wrong dear?" Anna asked.

"He hasn't called," Nellie said.

"He will. Don't worry," Anna said, stepping toward her and wiping her hands on a red and white checked apron. "He's called late before. Besides, he cannot tell you everything. I'm sure he has to keep some things secret." She reached out and brushed a strand of Nellie's hair from her face.

"You're probably right, but I think I should call someone, someplace," Nellie said as she slid one of the chairs away from the kitchen wall and sat down.

"Would you like some lunch?" Anna asked.

"I'm not hungry, thanks anyway," she said. She tapped her fingers on the tabletop.

"If you think it will make you feel better, there's the phone," Anna said, pointing to the dining room and the big wooden desk with the black phone setting on a corner.

Nellie pushed herself up from the table and, with indecision in her walk, went to the phone. She reached into the pocket of her black sport jacket, pulling a business card from it. On the back of it, Johnny wrote a number down for the Army Air Corps Reserve office in Pittsburgh. She dialed.

After two rings, a voice answered, "Army Air Corp, Captain Kiley speaking."

"Yes sir," Nellie said, nervously.

"My name is Nellie Bell from Oak Hill, West Virginia. My fiancé, John Roberts, is a member in your reserve unit out there and..."

"One moment ma'am," he said, "I'll have to put you on hold." Nellie waited. She tapped her fingernails on the wooden top of the desk, as noisy static droned in her ear.

Finally, the voice came back, "Are you next of kin, ma'am?"

"Next of kin?"

"Yes, ma'am."

"We are planning to get married," Nellie said. A growing lump in her thin throat made it hard to talk.

"Not next of kin then ma'am. Is that what you're saying?" The captain was firm and terse.

"We are going to get married. I need to know if you can put him in contact with me," she pleaded.

"Ma'am, it's our policy that, as a matter of security, we only provide information to the immediate family. I do not have your name listed on Captain Robert's contact information. One moment ma'am, can you hold?"

"Yes," she said. Frustration and anger, combined with fear, led her to close her eyes and bite her bottom lip.

"Hello ma'am," a voice crackled into the phone.

"Hello."

"This is Captain Robert's commander. I understand your concern and interest, but policy is policy. There is a war going on."

"Did something happen to Johnny?" Nellie demanded. There was a brief silence from the other end.

"Ma'am, I can't divulge that information to you."

"I'm his fiancée, dammit." Tears filled her eyes.

There was shuffling of paper in the phone, and then he said, "Miss Bell, this is totally against policy, but I can tell you this much. Captain Robert's did not arrive in Mobile. The military lists him as missing and unaccounted. That's all I can tell you, and that, ma'am, is more information than regulations allow."

* * *

Three weeks later, Johnny's sister called from Ohio. She told Nellie she received word from the Army that Johnny was gone. His plane had exploded somewhere over Tennessee. There were not any witnesses, but they knew he refueled in Kentucky. When he did not show up for a scheduled refueling in southern Tennessee, an aerial search had proved unsuccessful.

An old man held the key to the mystery when he showed up to sell a piece of metal from the plane for scrap. Around his neck were Johnny's dog tags. The dealer contacted the military. The wreckage was scattered across the rugged landscape. They found his chute, still packed and unopened. The hermit told the military he found the dog tags hanging in a tree. After three days of searching, they upgraded him from missing to dead.

She told Nellie she would sure like to meet her someday and that Johnny thought the world of her. Before she hung up, she said to her that if she was ever in Nelsonville to feel free to look her up.

Nellie carefully picked the wedding dress up from the bed. She turned it over in her hands and stroked the smooth satin with her fingers. She held a sleeve up to her cheek and brushed it across her cheekbone, thinking of how soft his hands were on her face. She slowly folded the dress up and crossed the hall.

The cedar hope chest that Uncle Jim had bought for Barbara when she was born sat catty corner against the wall. Nellie lifted the heavy lid until it rested on the wall and placed the dress, as carefully as if it was a baby, into the chest. The smell of cedar, heavy and musty, filled the little room. The evening light from the window shimmered on the satin.

She slowly twisted the diamond solitaire from her finger, gently placing it on top of the white satin. Reluctantly, she lowered the heavy lid as a ray of light from the window caught the diamond. It twinkled like a bright evening star. She looked at it and smiled, feeling his presence in the room. It was an omen, as if he were telling her to go on with strength. It twinkled one last time as she closed the lid. She did not know if it was the failing light causing the last sparkle, or if it was him. She locked the trunk and walked out of the room.

TWENTY
GOLDENROD AND GOLDEN YEARS

Nellie's retirement provided her with time for exploring Oak Hill. Today would be a good day to visit the cemetery, she decided. At the stoplight, she sat in the idling truck and looked around. The square convenience store on her right set in the same spot where the company store used to be. She remembered the night she and Cotton bought the tree in the lot. Now the progress of paving, and gas pumps, hid any sign of the Oak Hill that once was. Fifty-seven years had passed, evolving it with the kind of progress she disdained.

"All right, all right," she muttered. The impatient driver behind her honked again. "The damn light just changed," she said. She stomped her foot on the gas and the four-wheel drive Chevy truck chirped as the wheels grabbed the concrete. She passed a field of waist-high goldenrods with seed heads still yellow and swaying in the autumn breeze.

A glint of sunlight caught her eye, and in the middle of the field sat a half-buried rusted washtub, a haphazard monument to the miners once living in the row of company houses. The haunting emptiness of the field was very different from the days of laughing children, stickball, and clothes snapping on frayed lines. She smiled with fond remembrance. Past the washtub, a sign loomed over the yellow field: "Future Site of Wal-Mart."

Nellie turned the truck onto the gravel-covered road that led up to the cemetery. The tires chewed and crunched on the Brazil nut sized gravel as she slowed, seeing the familiar graves at the big oak tree. Parking near the tree, she stood leaning against the truck.

Across the rolling knolls of green, she looked past headstones large and small. Her right hand moved upward to shade her eyes from the bright sun as she scanned a section of the graveyard just to the right of the massive oak. The peeking headstone of river rock behind a slight rise beckoned her.

Years of weathering split the face of the red sandstone boulder. She kneeled slowly, her knees sinking in the soft grass and her bones feeling every bit of age in her years. Pulling some of the weeds from the front of the headstone, she paused to run her finger softly over the rough rock. She traced the only three remaining letters gently and with compassion. She remembered him as he was, before the war. The top of the stone provided balance as she pushed off with both hands to stand. A miniature American flag leaned crookedly on a wooden stick, and she bent to straighten it tenderly.

She looked down once more and shook her head at the thought of war, and how every night the television showed new young Cottons fighting in some place called Vietnam. She watched nightly as they read the numbers of young men killed each day, rolling numbers on the screen as mechanical as if it were a stock report.

"Such a waste of life," she murmured over the breeze. She knew there would be more wars, and death. The politics of the game required it.

Combing her fingers through her white hair, she looked out beyond Cotton's grave, and made her way across the cemetery toward a shining black granite marker. It loomed over three graves, one fresh and mounded with soil not yet sunk into the black ground.

Frankie lived to be nearly ninety, even with his lungs blackened from coal dust. Nellie remembered the years of useless treatment, and the countless trips to the hospital after Anna had passed away. Chills ran up her back as she thought of the nights she listened to him gasping, and then the silence. That awful silence sent her rushing to his side to shake him back to breathing.

Frankie had refused to sleep anywhere but on the couch since Anna died. He spit curses, begging Nellie just to let him die. A year and half ago he got his wish, in his sleep.

She looked at the middle grave of her mother, gone now for nearly twelve years. She suffered a stroke and never fully recovered. Nellie remembered her limping, her left side paralyzed: The crooked smile left by the stroke. The frustrated look on Anna's face when determination changed to surrender would always remain engraved on Nellie's mind.

The night Anna died, Nellie sat close to her on the couch in the parlor. She read passages from a Steinbeck novel. Anna interrupted her asking her to promise she would see to it that she rested eternally between the two men she admired most in her life. Nellie promised, not realizing that two days later she would have to keep it.

"Oh, Daddy," Nellie whispered, talking to the headstone to the left of Anna's, "You would have been very proud of me."

She ran her palm across the top of the smooth piece of stone, the slab of granite cold to her touch. She remembered him as if it was yesterday and reached up to brush a tear away. She looked at the graves one last time and walked back to her truck.

Nellie drove back to town, stopped at the convenience store, and bought a dozen eggs. She told the disinterested clerk how cheap they used to be when she was his age. Parking in front of her house, she noticed the fence leaned in the back yard. I will have to get that fixed soon, she thought, walking up onto the porch and noting the columns were also in bad need of painting. Inside, she put away the eggs, and went upstairs to nap.

Teetering on the precipice of sleep, the loud ring of the telephone interrupted her. In all the years, she never had a line installed upstairs: Instead claiming the exercise was good for her. She sleepily crawled from the bed. The rail of the banister on her palm guided her down the steep steps bathed in a dim yellow light. Suddenly, she pitched forward clawing at the railing. Her left shoulder struck the sharp edge of a step, and she tumbled to the bottom.

Curled at the bottom of the stairs, a sharp biting pain in her hip brought gasps with each attempt to reach the still ringing phone. She rolled slowly toward the small stand and grasped the curled black cord. The phone clattered to the floor. Blinding pain tore through her hip as she pulled the phone closer.

She spoke into the mouthpiece gasping out, "Hello, I..."

"What the hell took you so long?" The voice of Barbara's husband sounded far away. Nellie heard him exhale cigarette smoke.

"I fell," she winced with pain, and her voice broke between short gasps.

"When did this happen? Why didn't you call me?" Don said. "I'm always the last to know anything."

"Just now, Don. I fell just now." Nellie said. She held her hand tight on the hip area, wishing the burning pain would just go away.

"Oh? Did you call anybody?" he said.

Nellie sucked air through her clenched teeth.

"I told you... I... just did it," she said.

"Well, I'm in Dallas, so I'll hang up. Call someone," Don said.

There was a click and then a dial tone. She slid the old rotary phone close to her, and with a shaky finger tried to dial. Footsteps on the front porch caused a pause in her attempt. The mailbox slammed hollow, and Nellie forced out a cry. The mailman's steps grew distant and she tried again to call out, but her dry throat refused.

More footsteps sounded from the hall, moving quickly toward the back of the house. Maybe he heard her, she thought. She kept the front door locked, and the mailman knew she rarely locked the back door. Just yesterday, he used it to leave her a package. The backdoor slammed with a screech and the only sound was the dial tone left buzzing in her ear.

Fearing she would black out, she gained the strength to dial. A woman told her to stay on the line with her. The dim yellow bulb that poorly lit the steps spun crazily and sucked her in like a whirlpool into its black vortex.

* * *

Nellie woke to the blurry sight of a fat man and Barbara sitting at the bottom of her bed.

"Hello Mother," Barbara said. "I flew up from Dallas as soon as I heard you were getting a hip replacement."

The smell of garlic was still in Nellie's nostrils. She remembered the anesthesiologist telling her that could happen.

"Barbara, I hurt," she said, "See if they can give me something, please." Nellie lifted her arm up from the bed weakly and dropped it back down.

"I will Mother," she said. She nodded to her husband.

"Nellie, I'm sorry I had to meet you under these circumstances, but I'm Don," he said. He shuffled a handful of papers in his chubby hands.

Nellie barely heard him over the buzzing in her head. She thought he looked big and she thought his choice in ties was terrible, and then another pang of hot, burning pain tore through her. She breathed deep.

Don said, "Fortunately for you, I am an attorney. I'm concerned that you could lose everything you own." His eyes darted to Barbara, who seemed to be directing the script. She glanced at the papers in his hand and back to Nellie.

"Barbara, please. Please, tell them I need something," Nellie said, closing her eyes tight.

"In a minute mother, in a minute. Listen to what Donnie has to say," Barbara said. She spoke soft with false compassion.

"As I was saying, you are going to need some extended care after this, at least until you're able to get back on your feet." His pudgy fingers trembled and the papers nearly fell from his hands. He reached up and slid one finger between his collar and his fat, sunburned neck.

"You need to think about the cost of your care," he quickly added.

"I have insurance," Nellie replied. Her fingers trembled and she tried to roll.

"We know that, but not nearly enough. I've dealt with this many times. You need to protect your assets and the only way to do that is to sign them over to Barbara. That way they can't touch a thing. When you're all better, we simply transfer everything back to you," he said.

"It's in your best interest, Mother. I can't stay in Oak Hill, but I'd be glad to help you every day in Dallas. When you're better, I'll bring you back," Barbara said, reaching down and stroking the shin of Nellie's leg.

"You know I love you, I always have," Barbara whispered.

"My hip hurts so badly, Barbara. I really need something." Nellie gripped the sheets and grimaced as a tears rolled down her face.

"Sign the papers and I'll get the nurse. We need to help you, but if you won't help yourself, then I guess we'll just have to head back. The county can take care of you. You do remember the time Julia, the lady that worked with you, fell and the county took care of her. Must I remind you?" Barbara asked. Don looked at his watch impatiently.

Through the fog of her anesthetized brain, Nellie remembered Julia: How she had lost her home, the sight of her in the bed at the nursing home; so small and frail. She swore she would never let that happen to her.

"Poor Julia," she murmured, "Give me the pen."

Don held the papers flat on the bed as Nellie scrawled her name on the documents.

"There, the last one. Good. You'll be well taken care of Mother," he said. With both hands, he tapped the uneven edges of the sheaf on the top of his fat thigh, straightening the uneven edges. He glanced up to wink at a smiling Barbara.

Barbara rose from the chair and walked to the door.

"Nurse?" She watched the back of a white uniform moving away from her and down the hallway. "Nurse!" The young woman stopped suddenly, turned, and walked toward her. Barbara stepped back, allowing room for the nurse to walk into the room. She pointed to the bed.

"That's my Mommy there and she's in a terrible amount of pain. Give her something now. I can't believe this place," she said. She walked over to Don who was snapping his briefcase shut, and placed her hand on his shoulder.

"My wonderful hubby is a lawyer and I swear to God, I'll sue this place if she isn't given something right now." Barbara glared at the young woman.

"Yes, ma'am, I'll get her something," she said. Her clipboard quivered in her hands.

"Well, see to it," Barbara said. The nurse hurried from the room.

"Bye, Mother. We'll take care of everything."

Nellie lifted her head from the pillow and it weakly fell back sinking into the white pillowcase.

The two cons went directly to the courthouse and filed the deed. Within three weeks, they had auctioned off the house and all the furnishings. They saved a carton filled with a few of Nellie's personal items and enough clothes for a week. Barbara told her husband that her mother would not need much more. The nursing home just didn't have a lot of room and, besides, how much time did someone her age have left anyway?

Nellie's last view of West Virginia was from the jet that took the three of them to Texas. She spent days of painful therapy wondering where her daughter was, the daughter who had promised, just a month ago, to be by her side through all of this. Where was she now? The few short visits dwindled to none at all. Most of all, she missed her mountains and she missed her home.

She slipped in and out of her world. The pain from her hip replacement at times hurt more than it was worth, she thought. Was any of it worth it? She always knew where she was going in life regardless of the circumstances. Nellie always mapped out a course. However, this time she found herself without a map and without a plan.

TWENTY-ONE
FREEDOM AND FIREFLIES

The day finally arrived with the promise of a new life for Nellie. The years of surviving Beacon Manor drew closer to ending with each passing second. She felt new and alive, fueled with the healing power of her memories. She owed the transformation to her journal that revitalized and filled her former empty shell with hope.

She smiled remembering the conversations the nurses thought she did not hear. There were whispered words, like "impossible" and "miracle", thrown about the halls. The angry ones, unhappy with the tedium of care giving, spitefully peppered their sentences with contemptible remarks and then fought their way to the front of the paycheck line to be first: Those very same ones, who directed their conversations her way, saying, "She'll be carried out of here one day". To survive those days, she stubbornly lost herself in her strength-giving book of flowers.

There were the good ones though, she thought. The caring ones, who like angels, drifted on wings of white into the rooms at night. Their whispered good nights meant so much to her and the others. She could see their compassion because they wore it on their smiling faces. They became the only family for some in here. Elaina was one of them.

She pushed up from the chair and looked around the room. Her clock was no longer on the nightstand, but packed away in the small cardboard box that sat by the door. She walked across the room, passing the dust covered walker and stood at the doorway to the hall.

A new resident yelled from number ten, across the hall and to the left of her room. Screaming, angry curses echoed from behind the thin door. The non-stop racket appeared to shake the wooden door. Poor thing, she thought.

She decided to take one last walk around the halls of Beacon Manor: her victory lap. Elaina would be back soon with the tickets and this might be her last chance. She stepped into the hallway and turned right, past Banks' room. Through his open door, she watched him sleep. Time put away their differences, and when she realized that he could have been Cotton, she vowed to accept his cantankerous ways. Nellie tiptoed past the open doorway to the lounge.

The television played loudly in the lobby and the big woman sat eating an éclair. The chocolate was smeared around her mouth and bits of the filling hung from her chin. She sucked her fingers clean, briefly glancing up to look at Nellie, then back to the screen. The woman with the missing patches of hair sat strapped in her wheelchair, her fingers fiddling to free herself. She weakly picked repeatedly at the same knot. In all the years of watching her, Nellie knew her attempt was futile.

There was a sense of sadness that filled her as she walked back to her room. Guilt in wishing there was something she could do for them all. There was impossibility to her wish. She shook her head and concentrated on the blocks of tile passing under her feet.

Near Room 10, the woman screaming from within added the hammering thumps of her headboard against the thin walls. Nellie hurried past the closed door, and stopped only when she came to Martz's room. The sound of chalk on slate drifted to her ears. Light shone through the cracked door, and Nellie quietly pushed it open.

The chalkboard faced the teacher, and she worked the pastel chalk softly on the slate. Specks of chalk dust floated in the air, drifting onto her shoes. Her fingers switched colors with nimbleness, and her head moved back and forth from the window to the board. Pausing, she would look, then with a wet thumb, erase. When she stepped back, she left a drawing on the board looking like a photograph of the scene outside. Nellie smiled and pulled the door shut.

Back in her room, she sat in her chair and reached for the burnt orange curtains, sliding them open wide. It was an overcast day: the sky just a shade or two below black. The crape myrtles were taller and fuller since her first day here, more than three years ago. At least they had more branches, she thought.

Farther out in the parking lot, taillights caught her attention. She studied the big silver car as the driver stopped before turning onto the main road. It looked like Barbara's big Cadillac. Surely, she would not visit her now, unless she had gotten wind of the money. My eyes must be playing tricks on me, she thought.

Nellie leaned her head back into the cushion of the chair and rested her eyes. She had not slept well last night with the excitement of leaving. The visions of Oak Hill filled her head, and she knew the things she wanted to do when she got back there. She wanted to show Elaina everything. She would try to find the beech tree and see if the initials and heart were still there. They would go to the cemetery and put flowers on the graves. Galloway had already begun the paperwork for buying the land her Daddy once owned and Nellie intended to build a house on the very same spot.

She would show Elaina the school she first attended and show her where Cornpone's shack once stood. She might even trace the routes of her old moonshine runs. They were going to have fun, that was for sure. Nellie was ready for fun, ready for life. This time she would really live it and not worry about a dime.

The director of nursing poked her head in the door. Nellie opened her eyes when she spoke.

"Miss Bell, they need you at administration to sign some papers."

Nellie stood on shaking legs. The moment had arrived that would legally break the bonds.

"I'm ready," Nellie said.

"I'll walk with you," replied the nurse.

The woman in Room 10 continued her cursing. Only when Nellie stepped into the administrator's office and the door closed did the ranting woman's voice appear muffled.

"Have a seat, Miss Bell," a balding man in a gray tweed sport coat said. He shifted his weight in the squeaking leather chair and rolled it until his elbows rested on the large wooden desk. The shuffling of papers, as he organized them, echoed in Nellie's ears. Finally, the silence was broken when he cleared his throat.

"Sign on the lines marked with an X," he said, immediately going back to another stack of papers. When she was satisfied that they were for her discharge, she signed each one.

While she wrote, she overheard the man telling the nurse about the new resident in number ten.

"These are her papers here," he said, tapping the stack. He appeared anxious to dispose of them.

"She is very belligerent and difficult. She is not happy with her hip replacement. She will be here for a while. I need you to set up a therapy program." The nurse took the papers from him and went out the door.

"Here you are," Nellie said, sliding the papers across the desk

He picked up the papers and looked them over giving her a copy of each one as he finished with the original.

"Is someone picking you up?" he asked.

"Yes, sir. Elaina Adams should be here soon. She's getting our tickets from the airport."

"Very good then," he said "you can wait in your room if you like. Just remember, as of this moment you are completely released of our responsibility, so don't get into any trouble while you wait for her," he said, giving her a kidding wink. He reached across the desk and extended his hand.

"Bye now, Miss Bell, and good luck."

"Thank you," she said.

On the way back to her room, the noise from the woman in Room 10 grew louder. Nellie stopped at her door, and knowing the pain of the therapy the new patient would be going through, thought it might be a kind gesture to fill her in. She turned and looked at the door, paused, and checked up and down the halls. She opened the door and stepped inside. The door closed with a metallic click.

Nellie turned facing the woman who lay on her side in the dark room. The woman picked at the bottom of the drawn shade. Nellie moved slowly and quietly to the side of the woman's bed. She looked at the hair on the back of her head and thought she couldn't be fifty, no more than sixty at the most.

"Hello there," Nellie said, softly.

"Who the hell are you?" the woman replied without turning.

"My name's Nellie, I had to go through the same..."

The woman rolled to face her. A blanket clutched in her hands and drawn tight below her eyes hid her face. She struggled to reach the lamp on the nightstand. Nellie reached out and turned the switch. The woman looked at Nellie with piercing gray eyes filled with contempt. Her lip curled in a snarl and she screamed, "Listen bitch, I don't need your..."

"Barbara!" Nellie said. She took two steps quickly back from the edge of the bed.

"Well Mother, I bet you're happy now. You finally got even," she said. Her wrinkled face twisted into a mask of contempt.

"Even?" Nellie asked. She backed up a few more steps, seeing Barbara struggling to rise from the bed.

"Well, dear Mother, I'm sure you figured out by now that I had Don make the call that sent you sailing down the steps. I hid across the hall and waited. I pushed you Mother," she snapped.

Nellie stared at her. So, I wasn't crazy, she thought.

"And Mother," Barbara hissed, "I wanted you dead. The mailman foiled that, so I ran out the back door."

"But why, Barbara. I'm your mother," Nellie asked.

"Donnie had connections in banking Mother, he knew the class action suit was filed long ago. Long before you did, and with you gone, I would be heir to it all."

Nellie looked at the evil woman and turned, walking out of the room.

"Mother," Barbara screamed, "I'm not finished with you." Nellie closed the door behind her, shutting out the words.

In her room, Nellie reached down into the cardboard box. She moved aside the clock and underneath her neatly folded dresses pulled out the book of pressed flowers. She set the book on the floor as she rummaged through the box until she found an empty cough drop box. She carefully slid the cellophane off, picked up the book, and went to her chair.

She pulled the knotted string hanging from the back of her flower book. Gingerly, she removed the pills one at a time. When the last one dropped into the cellophane, she twisted it. Returning the book to the safety of the box, she held the pills in her hand hiding them behind her when Elaina came into the room, smiling and waving the tickets.

"I got them, Miss Nellie. It's time to go. Are you ready?" Elaina asked, fidgeting with excitement.

"In one minute. I'll be right back," Nellie said. She walked out her door and across the hall to Room 10, and went inside.

"Barbara?" she asked.

"Yes, Mother, I knew you'd come back. I know exactly how you are. You need me and now I'm here," she said arrogantly.

"Here darling," Nellie said. Barbara rolled just enough to reach with an open hand. Nellie dropped the cellophane wrapper into her hand and said, "You might need these. It can get crazy around here. I know that because of you."

Nellie turned and marched out the door shutting it tightly behind her. Elaina walked into the hallway hugging the cardboard box close to her chest.

"Let's go," Nellie said.

Barbara's voice thundered down the hallway waking up Banks.

"Hey pipe down. You'll give away our position."

Nellie paused a moment and waited. From the distance, like clockwork, she heard "To the principal's office, young lady."

***

A few months later back in Oak Hill, the townsfolk celebrated the founding of Oak Hill. Nellie and Elaina sat on the porch of the new house looking out over the town. The fireworks soared up from the celebration and splashed the night sky with color so close she felt she could reach out and touch them. It's beautiful, she thought, lifting a glass of the cold mint tea to her lips.

Elaina stood up yelling, "Kareena, it's time for the finale."

Kareena ran from the back yard and bounded up the steps, her ruffled dress bouncing and a broad smile on her face. She climbed up into Nellie's lap and snuggled her face into her chest.

The finale started and rockets of every sort lit the sky. Nellie looked out across the valley and then she felt the small hand tugging on the front of her blouse. She looked down at Kareena.

"These are for you. I picked them today, Grammy," Kareena said.

Nellie lowered her head for a closer look. In that moment, a huge burst of white light from the finale of the fireworks lit up the entire porch and Nellie clearly made out the small bouquet of bluebells held for her by the little girl.

In the light of the fireworks, and as the voices of celebration drifting up from the town below, two other voices chimed in: From the corner of the porch, Gordon Banks dressed in his uniform yelled, "Viva La France" and Gertie Martz rocked in a chair near him and said, "God Bless America."

Later that night, Nellie placed several of the flowers Kareena had given to her in the last page of her book. Underneath it, she wrote slowly and deliberately, one word: "Freedom," and closed the embroidered cover.

ABOUT THE AUTHOR

Ronnie Ray Jenkins (1957-) was raised in the Appalachians of Pennsylvania. Born, one of eleven children of a coal miner, Jenkins brings a new voice, and narration in his works. Gritty, to the point, and at times, humorous, many of his works deal with the struggles of the Appalachian common folk. He has authored three novels, and two collections of short stories. He is currently working on his next novel.

www.ronnierayjenkins.com

12043644R00099

Made in the USA
Charleston, SC
07 April 2012